Quasar and the Eye of the Serpent

By
T. K. Reed

iUniverse, Inc.
New York Bloomington

iUniverse books may be ordered through booksellers or by contacting:

iUniverse
1663 Liberty Drive
Bloomington, IN 47403
www.iuniverse.com
1-800-Authors (1-800-288-4677)

Because of the dynamic nature of the Internet, any Web addresses or
links contained in this book may have changed since publication and
may no longer be valid. The views expressed in this work are solely those
of the author and do not necessarily reflect the views of the publisher,
and the publisher hereby disclaims any responsibility for them.

ISBN: 978-1-4401-2751-9 (sc)
ISBN: 978-1-4401-2753-3 (dj)
ISBN: 978-1-4401-2752-6 (ebook)

Library of Congress Control Number: 2009923629

Printed in the United States of America

iUniverse rev. date: 03/27/2009

For Mom, Dad, my husband, and my children

Acknowledgments

I wrote this book to show my children that anything is possible if you believe in yourself and if you have the desire to accomplish what you set out to do. I wish to thank them and my husband for supporting and believing in me.

Contents

Chapter One

The Light

In a land far, far away from any townspeople, there lay a small country cabin tucked away deep inside the forest. In the cabin lived a family whose surname was Robert. Their family consisted of a father, a daughter, and a son. The boy's name was Mathew, and the girl's name was Sue. Mathew was very tall for his age of fourteen, for he was close to six feet now and handsome. He was skinny and had long, scraggly dark hair that went to his shoulders, and crystal-blue eyes. His nose and face were thin. Sue, on the other hand, wasn't so tall for thirteen: she was just over five feet tall. She too had dark hair, but it was straight and very long and tidy. She kept it pulled back in a long braid. She also had blue eyes, a slender face, and a thin nose. Like Mathew, she was very skinny.

Mathew and Sue used to play a lot. Since it was just the two of them, they always played after dinner. They always had to help father clean up the dinner dishes and put things away. Then off they would scurry to enjoy what they liked most.

"Tag, you're it!" shouted Mathew to Sue, just as soon as they got off the back porch.

"That's not fair! I wasn't ready!" Sue screamed irritably.

"You're just mad because I tagged you first!"

Sue ran at Mathew in a fury and chased him around the picnic table, and then around the very large ash tree that was in the yard, until finally they headed toward the forest.

"Mathew, you're not playing fair!" screamed Sue, as she stumbled over a large tree root sticking out of the ground. "Slow down; you know I can't run that fast! I just hurt my big toe!" Sue sat down on the ground and took her shoe and sock off and began to rub her big toe. Mathew came back and sat down on the ground next to her, panting.

"How's your toe, Sis?" Mathew asked sincerely.

"Well, if you really cared, you'd rub it for me."

"Are you crazy?" laughed Mathew. "I'm not going to rub your foot. It stinks!" Mathew crinkled up his nose and pinched it shut with his fingers.

"It does not stink!" cried Sue, as she pulled up her sock and slipped her foot into her shoe. "Tag, you're it!" shouted Sue, as she slapped Mathew on the back. She sprang up like a rabbit and ran as fast as she could.

"Hey, you cheated!" yelled Mathew, as he took off like a bullet.

"I'm just paying you back!" Sue jumped over a big, hollow log.

The children played like this for hours. Each one tagged the other until they had gone farther into the forest than they had ever been before.

"What's wrong, Sue?" asked Mathew.

"I think we're lost. Do you know how to get back to the house?" asked Sue worriedly.

"Well of course I do. Don't worry." Mathew was a year older; he always took care of his little sister. As they started their journey back home, they spotted a glowing light in the distance.

"Do you see that?" asked Sue. She rubbed her eyes as if they weren't working properly.

"Yeah, I do. I wonder what it is. Let's go check it out!" answered Mathew.

As they continued to walk, it seemed they were not getting any closer to the light. "This is weird," said Sue. "We aren't any closer to it than when we first saw it."

"I know," said Mathew who was just as mystified as Sue.

"I wonder," Mathew said, scratching his head, "Whether zigzagging back and forth to the light would make any difference. We've been walking in a straight line and we're still not there."

"We could try," replied Sue, who had been scratching her head as if she had fleas.

As they walked back and forth stepping over briars, dead trees, and poison ivy, they could see that the light was getting closer to them. They saw a tall figure wearing a black top hat and black trench coat. He was holding a lantern. The children stopped walking.

"Who could that be in the middle of a forest? There's no one around for miles. And why would he be holding a lantern?" asked Sue. "It's not dark yet."

It was true, it wasn't dark yet, but it would be in a few hours, and they still hadn't figured out how to get out of the forest and back home.

"Maybe he could help us out of here if we asked him," said Sue who was looking up at Mathew, hoping that he would not agree.

"That's a good idea. Let's go!" He started walking again.

"I was just joking! We're not supposed to talk to strangers," said Sue, as she grabbed him by the shoulder and pulled him back. "How many times has father said that to us?"

"Sue," Mathew turned to face his sister and planted his hands on her shoulders. "We're lost. We have no other choice. We have to see if he can tell us how to get home."

"I'm scared, Mathew." A tear slid down Sue's face.

Mathew was scared too, but he couldn't show it. He had to be strong for both of them. He forced a slight smile onto his face, took Sue's hand, and, together, they started to walk once again toward the strange figure.

As they approached, the man didn't appear to move. He stood straight up, shoulders back, and looked straight ahead in another direction; his thin face was motionless and stern. His coal-black, stringy hair stuck out from underneath his black top hat. He had a black mustache with a black goatee.

"Excuse me, Sir," said Mathew as they stopped a few feet in front of him. "Excuse me!" He said again trying to get the man's attention.

The man looked first at Mathew and then at Sue with his dark sunken eyes. His thick bushy eyebrows stuck out from just under the brim of his hat. He lowered the lantern to get a better look.

"Where have you been? You are late. You should have been here hours ago!" The man glanced down at his time piece. "We must go! We must go, now!" said the man sternly. He turned and started to walk very fast.

The children thought this to be very odd. Why had this man obviously been expecting us?

They did not know this man. To learn more, they immediately began pursuing him.

"What do you mean, we're late? Have you been expecting us, Sir?" asked Sue, a little out of breath.

"Yes, I've been expecting you, but now we must hurry. We haven't much time!" said the man, who was now moving at a much faster speed.

"But Sir, could you tell us why you've been expecting us? You see, we're lost and ..."

"Lost?" laughed the man. "Lost? I know exactly where you are!" The man laughed again, and continued on his way.

"Well, you may know where we are, but we do not. We must get back home because father will be worried," Sue panted as she and Mathew were now running along side the stranger, jumping over obstacles to keep up.

"Your father will be fine. He will not miss you."

"What do you mean by that?" asked Mathew, harshly. "Do you know our father? How do you know he will not miss us? Did you hurt him?" asked Mathew, grabbing at the man's arm. "*Stop!*" yelled Mathew.

The man came to a complete halt with the children almost colliding into him. They looked into the sunken eyes of this stranger with complete confusion and terror imbedded in their faces. "Like I said before, your father will not be worried, and he will be fine. You will have to believe me," said the man, as he started on his way again.

"We aren't coming with you!" Mathew cried. "We have to get home, and if you can't help us then we'll just have to go it alone." And with that, Mathew grabbed Sue's hand and pulled her in another direction. They were going to find their way out.

The man ran after them, however. "Please come back with me," he pled. This time, he was struggling to keep up with them. "We need your help. You two are the only ones who can help us!"

The children looked into the man's face and saw that he was sincere, and with the forest growing ever so dark, they would never find their way out without this man's help.

"Fine, then," said Mathew. "Tell us everything. We need to know what's going on. Then we'll decide if we want to help you or not!"

"I can't tell you, but Quasar will tell you everything that you need to know."

"Who is Quasar? And why can't you tell us?" asked Sue skeptically.

"Quasar is the Great Wolf. He is the leader of all the wolves. He has very powerful magic, or he used to."

"What do you mean, used to?" asked Mathew.

"A witch, who was jealous of the Great Wolf's power, cursed him and now he is enclosed in this"—the man's voice dropped to a whisper—"this, unspeakable prison."

"And why are we here?" asked Sue. "What are we supposed to do about it? We don't know anything about magic or about this wolf."

"But you do have magic. You are the ones who will release the Great Wolf and restore his power," the stranger told them.

"Why us?" asked Mathew.

"So it is written in *The Book of Wisdom*," replied the man.

"*The Book of Wisdom?*" asked Sue, looking at Mathew, who shrugged his shoulders.

"I can't tell you anymore. Please come with me. The Great Wolf will explain everything." The stranger then held out his hands to the children. They both grabbed a hand, and then it happened.

The ground opened up, and they were falling, falling, and falling into a pitch-black pool of nothing. It felt like they were falling forever.

When are we going to stop? Where are we going to be when we stop? Are we going to stop? The questions kept popping into the children's heads. *What's happening?*

Then all of a sudden it was light again. The children and the man were back in the forest, and it seemed to be early morning, for the sun glistened through the gaping leaves, and the dew dripped as if new. The forest was full of creatures. Mathew could hear the birds singing; he saw rabbits scurrying to get back into their holes and squirrels jumping into trees to get back into their nests. As they looked around, there it was: the wolf. What a horrific sight. It seemed to have been turned into a statue, but only halfway. On one side of the body he was a wolf covered with beautiful grey, brown, and white fur. His face was outlined with snowy white fur. He had an upright, fully furred ear, a bright blue-crystal eye, and a long snout. His two legs looked very strong and powerful. His tail was robust, long, and bushy. On the other side, however, there was only decay. There was an eye socket, but no eyeball; there was no flesh or fur: only bone. You could see his rib cage, his heart, lungs, and other organs, but they had been turned into stone. His heart did not beat, nor did his lung or kidney move. The poor creature was half living and half dead.

Mathew moved Sue behind him, as if he could protect her from this horrific sight. She laid her head on Mathew's shoulder to hide her eyes, but she saw what an evil person the witch must be to have inflicted such a curse upon such an extraordinary beast.

7

Chapter Two

Quasar

Good morning," said the wolf. "You must be Mathew and Sue Robert. Is that so?"

"Why yes it is, but how did you know?" asked Mathew in amazement.

Mathew and Sue walked closer to the wolf so they could better hear what he had to say. Sir Wilfred stood beside the wolf.

"I sent Sir Wilfred to fetch you. I felt your presence in the forest," said the wolf.

"You felt our presence?" asked Sue. "And how exactly do you feel our presence?" She moved out from behind Mathew.

"I'm sure that Sir Wilfred has explained everything?" asked the wolf, looking reassuringly at Sir Wilfred.

"No! He has not!" exclaimed Mathew. "The only thing he told us is that we're supposed to help you break the spell that some old witch put on you and something about a *Book of Wisdom*, but we don't know why we have to do this. He keeps saying that our father will not miss us, and that he won't worry. What is that supposed to mean? I'm sure he is worrying right this minute!"

"Master Quasar, if I may speak?" asked Sir Wilfred graciously.

"Yes, you may," said the wolf, as he smiled half a smile.

"I recollect, did you not ask me not to reveal too much? Did I understand you correctly, Master?" asked Sir Wilfred.

"Yes, you did well Sir Wilfred," said the wolf reassuringly.

"Can we get on with this?" asked Mathew. "I want to know why we're here and why we can't go home!" His face was growing redder by the minute. Sue stood beside Mathew with her arms crossed, tapping her foot impatiently.

"These grounds," began the wolf, ignoring Mathew's temper, "that we are standing upon belonged to the royal family. I used to provide magic to the only child of the royal family. The King and Queen had wanted children so bad. After several failed pregnancies they finally gave birth to a beautiful baby girl, but she was very frail and sickly when she was born, so the royals came to me for healing magic. They had heard of this so-called all-powerful wolf that could perform amazing magical tasks, so they came to me. We came to an understanding that in return for my services, they allowed my pack and I to live in the woods. We were protected from human hunters and we could eat whatever we wanted. We had a very good arrangement, until the witch betrayed me."

"What do you mean by that?" asked Sue. She and Mathew sat on the ground in front of the wolf to better hear his story.

"The witch," continued the wolf "became very jealous. She wanted me to take precious crystals and jewels from the royals so that she could work some of her dark magic and so she could satisfy her greed. You see, she was very jealous of me. She could not perform her magic as I could. Plus, I had access to the things that I needed to do my magic."

"How did you know that we were in the forest and what are names were?" interrupted Mathew.

"A good question," said the wolf. "I've known of you for a very long time. I knew your mother, and I can sense your presence when you are in the forest. That is why I sent Sir Wilfred to fetch you."

"You knew our mother?" asked Sue who gave Mathew a quick look and then looked back at the wolf.

"Yes, I knew her when she was a child. She grew up in the forest and liked to play here. I saw her many times."

"What else do you know of our Mother?" queried Mathew.

"I have not the time to tell you everything that I know of your Mother, only that you will see her again," said Quasar."

"How is that possible?" asked Mathew. "Our Mother is dead! Why should we believe you?" This could be some kind of trick!" said Mathew hatefully.

"I assure you that your Mother is very much alive," said Quasar, and he continued, "I would not trick you."

"What is this *Book of Wisdom* that Sir Wilfred mentioned to us?" asked Mathew.

"Ah, yes, *The Book of Wisdom*. This book has been handed down for thousands of years, from generation to generation. This book contains the secrets of many spells. It tells you exactly what you need and how to perform each spell," the wolf answered graciously.

"Oh, and I guess it said that you needed two kids to break any spell that a witch casts onto a wolf, is that right?" asked Mathew sarcastically.

"Well yes," the wolf answered, ignoring Mathew's sarcasm. "But I also need you to fetch the things that I need to perform the magic to break the spell. May I please have your word that you both will help me?"

"You still haven't answered all of our questions," said Sue. "What about our father? Sir Wilfred says that he won't miss us. What does that mean? Why won't he miss us?"

"It simply means that it should only take twenty-four hours to gather everything we need to break the spell. When you have finished, you will return home at the exact moment you went into the forest. Your father will never know you left. I should also mention that you have already wasted four hours of your twenty-four hours; I'm sure Sir Wilfred told you that you were already late. So if there are no other questions, shall we move along to the task at hand?" The wolf had a slight smirk on his face.

"What do we do first?" asked Mathew, who was intrigued by the idea of a quest.

"Does this mean that you will help me?" asked the wolf.

"I don't see as we have a choice," said Mathew. Sue nodded in reluctant agreement.

"You always have a choice," said Quasar. "If you do not choose to help, I will understand and will allow you to go home."

"Do you mean that?" asked Sue hopefully.

"Well of course!" said the wolf. "I cannot make you help me. You must be willing to help in order to break the curse."

Sue looked at Mathew; they quickly turned their backs on the wolf and Sir Wilfred in order to make their decision.

"We can just go home and be with father again. Let's just go!" whispered Sue very excitedly.

"But Sue we can't just leave. Look at that poor creature. If we can make a difference we should stay and try," said Mathew.

"Are you crazy? This is not our doing. We didn't cause this. This is not our concern."

"I know we didn't do this, but we can fix it. We can free the wolf from his curse. Would you want to live like that?" asked Mathew.

"Well, no. But we don't even know what we'll have to do," said Sue, looking at the wolf.

"The wolf will tell us. We just have to do what he says. How hard can it be?" asked Mathew convincingly. "We will be home with father in less than twenty hours. We need to get started right away. He also knows our mother. Maybe he can tell us more about her. Maybe she is alive."

"Mathew, our Mother is dead," said Sue looking very sad.

"Sue we don't know that for sure. Father never spoke of her. He has always been very vague about her even when we would ask questions. We should find out more and this is our chance," said Mathew very convincingly.

"Alright!" said Sue reluctantly.

"Alright, we'll help," said Mathew as they turned around.

"Do both of you agree?" asked the wolf.

Sue nodded her head yes.

"Alright then, we'll get started. *The Book of Wisdom*," the wolf continued, "states that in order for this spell to be broken, we must have six magical objects. These objects include herbs, crystals, and other things related to magic. I can only tell you where the first one is located. When you get there, you will have to answer a riddle or solve a puzzle to find the next object."

"Oh, come on! We're not here to play games! What if we don't know how to solve the problem or puzzle? Then what?" Mathew already felt frustrated, and they hadn't even begun.

"Then you will fail," said the wolf. "But I know you are not failures. You will not think of yourselves as failures, and I know that you will not fail me. So believe in yourselves, and use your heads, and you will succeed. May I continue?" asked the wolf, looking at Mathew with his one good eye.

"Yes, you may," said Sue, giving Mathew the evil eye.

"I cannot tell you what it is that you are looking for, but only that it is located down inside the Earth in Mount Lacuna. Once inside Mount Lacuna, you will find worker dwarfs inside mining this precious mineral. As I said before, you will have to answer a riddle or solve a puzzle in order to find the next task. Only then will you be rewarded with the magical object. Do you understand the instructions?" asked the wolf with a blank face.

"And just how are we supposed to get to this Mount Lacuna? I don't know where it is and we have no way of getting there," said Mathew, looking gravely bewildered.

"You do not have to travel alone. Sir Wilfred will accompany you on your journey. He will take you where you need to go," replied the wolf.

"So that's it? This is all that you're going to tell us?" asked Mathew, who was pacing back and forth. He almost walked into Sue, who was also pacing back and forth.

"This is all I am allowed to tell you; if I say more, you will be unable to break the spell. Now you must go. You have wasted another hour; only nineteen remain. Go Sir Wilfred, may your travels be free of burden and sorrow," said the wolf.

As Sir Wilfred motioned for the children to grab onto his hands, Sue asked, "What did he mean by burden and sorrow?"

Chapter Three
The Book of Wisdom

As they dropped down into the earth once more, it felt like they were spinning out of control into total darkness. It seemed much longer this time. Sue and Mathew could not see each other; they could only feel each other's hands. Finally, after what seemed to be two to three minutes, they landed with a thud. Sue fell on her ankle, which felt as though she had sprained it, and Mathew fell hard on his behind. Sir Wilfred, of course, fell gracefully.

"I don't know if I can walk," said Sue as she bent down to rub her ankle. Sir Wilfred pulled what seemed to be a stick out of his jacket pocket and touched Sue's ankle with it.

"How does it feel now?" asked Sir Wilfred with concern.

"It feels much better," she said, wiggling her foot. "But how did you do that?"

"Never mind; we must get going." Sir Wilfred returned the stick to his jacket pocket and then helped Sue onto her feet.

As Mathew dusted himself off, he looked around. *What an odd looking place*, he thought. It was much more open than the forest.

The terrain was flat with mountains in every direction. Mathew had never been out of the forest and he had never seen such large mountains. He truly was in awe. He noticed that one mountain was even bigger than the rest.

"That must be Mount Lacuna," said Mathew, pointing at the tallest one.

"Yes," said Sir Wilfred, "Come along."

"But how are we going to get up there?" asked Sue, who was rubbing her ankle to remind Sir Wilfred of her fall.

"We must walk very fast," said Sir Wilfred, who bent down to check on Sue's ankle. "Does it still hurt?" he asked.

"No, but..."

"Then let's go!" said Sir Wilfred, cutting Sue off. "We mustn't waste time," and off Sir Wilfred went, almost jogging. Sue and Mathew turned and looked at each other and then started after Sir Wilfred.

"Do you mean to tell us that we are going to physically walk up this mountain when all you have to do is take us there using magic?" asked Sue.

"Yes!" said Sir Wilfred, without stopping.

With that, the children followed Sir Wilfred up the mountain. They stepped over small rocks and climbed over big boulders. The children caught glimpses of creatures scurrying under rocks for cover. One creature had the tail and body of a snake, but the head of a cricket. Mathew rubbed his eyes gently, thinking that he must be seeing things, and shook his head in disbelief. *Surely that wasn't so*, he thought to himself. Sue on the other hand saw a newt that was green and looked like a salamander. When she looked again, it had the head of a spider with pinchers and all. Sue looked at

Mathew to see if he had seen it, but his head was turned in the other direction.

The trees that the children saw were also different; they had faces, which seemed to smile as they walked past. Their roots, which poked out from the ground, sank into the ground right before they came through. It was as though the trees were preventing them from tripping.

The foliage was also strange. The children noticed that as they walked close, the leaves on the plants curled and uncurled as they passed. Sue and Mathew looked at each other and shrugged their shoulders.

Mathew bent down to touch a plant that had small strawberries growing on it, and the plant snapped at his hand. Then it seemed to realize that this boy was special and graciously extended a strawberry toward him. Mathew picked two strawberries and handed one to Sue. She thanked the plant before eating it.

The children saw strange creatures flying in the air. They looked up and caught a glimpse of a large bird or beast in the air. It had very large, white wings with long strong legs, and it resembled a horse. *Could it be a Pegasus?* Thought Sue. Though she had never seen one in real life, she had read about them in fairy tales. *Could they really exist? No! Surely not,* she thought and shook her head.

The climb wasn't that bad, but they were getting hungry.

"Do you have any food? We're starved," Sue asked Sir Wilfred. She was really having trouble keeping up.

"I do have some beef jerky, if you both would like some?" replied Sir Wilfred.

"Yes, we are both very hungry," said Mathew.

Sir Wilfred reached inside his jacket and pulled out a black pouch. He opened it up and pulled out two big pieces of beef jerky.

He handed one to Sue and one to Mathew. They both started to eat and immediately began to feel full and energized with each bite they took. Sue wondered if this jerky had some sort of magical herbs in them for it to work this quickly. Sir Wilfred tore off a piece for himself and closed the bag. He put it back inside his shirt and started to walk briskly again. They walked for another hour or so when the children began to hear voices, along with whistling and singing. Both children hurried to catch up with Sir Wilfred.

"Are we there?" asked Sue anxiously.

"It's just on the other side of those trees," replied Sir Wilfred. And with that said, the two children took off at a run. When they got to the trees, they came to a screeching halt. There they saw hundreds of dwarfs that all looked alike. The children were looking down on a valley of worker dwarfs going in and out of a mine. They were short and stocky and had small, beady eyes, long white beards, and short, stubby noses with rose-colored cheeks. Their ears were somewhat big for their bodies. They wore short black pants that came to their knees, long-sleeved green shirts, and black boots that were covered with dust. They wore grey gloves that protected their hands. The dwarfs had dust on their noses, cheeks, and legs. As the children watched the little people, Sir Wilfred came up behind them.

"You must now go into the mine. I will wait for you," said Sir Wilfred.

As they made their way down to the mine, they continued to watch the dwarfs running around. The dwarfs were working just outside of the mine. Some were pushing little mine carts that seemed to be filled with nothing. One dwarf was in the front, pulling, and another dwarf was in the back, pushing, and they seemed to be straining. They would then dump the empty cart on the ground just outside the mine and then back into the mine they would go with the cart. Then, other dwarfs set to work with their pickaxes, breaking apart what seemed to be nothing. They were working very hard, for they had sweat above their brows and were continuously pulling out handkerchiefs from their back pockets to wipe their foreheads. Sue and Mathew looked at each other in disbelief.

"Can you see what they're mining?" Mathew whispered to Sue.

"No, I don't see anything."

As they entered the mine, they could see what looked like torches along the perimeter that lit the mine up pretty well once their eyes had adjusted. The dwarfs dumped their empty carts in the middle of this huge cave, and other dwarfs were working hard with their pickaxes. The dwarfs had made what appeared to be a scaffold, a raised platform along one wall of the cave, which was several stories high. There was a dwarf on each floor of the scaffold and each floor had a crate that was attached to a pulley with ropes. The dwarfs would fill the crate with what appeared to be nothing, and then it was lowered down to the very bottom of the cave to where other dwarfs were unloading the crates into their carts. Then, the crates could be hoisted back up the scaffolding, so that it could be refilled. Then the dwarfs would wheel the carts to the middle of the cave, or to just outside the cave, and dump the carts.

"They're certainly not afraid of hard work," Mathew whispered to Sue.

There was one main dwarf to whom the other dwarfs reported. The main dwarf wore the same clothes as the others, except he sported a red-and-white-striped cap on his head. He also had a pencil behind his ear and one in his hand, along with a book that he was writing in. Because this dwarf looked somewhat important, Mathew and Sue decided to approach him.

"Excuse me, Sir. Excuse me. We were told to come here in search of some kind of magical object," said Sue, as she tapped him on the shoulder to get his attention.

The dwarf did not respond; he was too busy trying to write down something that another dwarf was telling him.

"Excuse me, Sir," Sue said again.

"I'll be right with you!" screeched the dwarf, and he continued writing.

"Now what is it?" asked the dwarf as he turned around, sporting a disgusted look on his face. He looked up at the children. "You're late!" he said, pointing and shaking a pencil at them. "You were supposed to be here hours ago!"

"We know," said Mathew, "but we couldn't help it."

"Couldn't help it!" mocked the dwarf. "Do you know how many times a day I hear that?" We couldn't help it!" shrieked the dwarf again mockingly.

"Well, we couldn't!" said Sue sternly. She crossed her arms and nodded her head.

"Well, let's get on with it, now that you are here!" said the dwarf. He turned his back on the children and flipped through the book that he was writing in. He stopped and read a few pages and then turned back around to the children.

"First off, you are the Robert children, correct?" asked the dwarf.

"Yes," said Sue and Mathew together.

"And you are here to gather the objects to help the Great Wolf, correct?" continued the dwarf.

"Yes," said the children.

"Then here is your riddle." The dwarf read from his notebook, in a loud, clear voice.

"I represent light and energy.
My color is of royal descent.
I have been used for centuries by soothsayers.
What am I?"

The children turned to each other with blank faces. Sue looked back at the dwarf. "Could you repeat that again?"

The dwarf's eyebrow went up, but he repeated the riddle as he gazed into the children's eyes. The children started to repeat the riddle several times in their heads.

"Well this doesn't seem too hard to figure out," Mathew said finally. "We already know that we need a crystal. Years ago the color purple was used by the royals, and soothsayers used crystal balls. So all we need to know is what crystal is purple?"

"That's easy," said Sue.

"It's amethyst!" They both said and at that moment, the mine lit up, and they could see the amethyst crystals sticking out of the walls of the mine, glowing brightly. It was beautiful. They looked up at the dwarf.

"Very good!" said the dwarf, with a smile on his face. "Here is your crystal." The dwarf handed Sue an amethyst crystal in the shape of a triangle; it filled the palm of her hand.

"Now that was easy," said the dwarf. "The clues will get harder as you go, but *The Book of Wisdom* is yours to use throughout your journey." He handed Mathew a big, black book covered with ancient writing. He also gave Mathew a piece of puzzle. "You will receive a piece of puzzle for every object that you collect. Once you have all the pieces of the puzzle that you need, fit them together. Something magical will happen."

The children turned around to walk out of the mine. They looked up and saw Sir Wilfred standing at the mouth of the mine where they had left him. When they reached him, they turned and looked at the dwarfs that were still loading, pulling, pushing and dumping the carts. They noticed that the carts were no longer empty. They were filled with amethyst crystals. Some were large clusters, some had one point, and some had more. They saw where they were dumping the carts of crystals, and the piles were enormous. The crystals exuded so much energy that Sue and Mathew could actually feel a tingling sensation on their bodies and skin. The children showed Sir Wilfred the crystal, the book, and the piece of puzzle.

"Very good," he said, nodding his head. "What is your next clue?" The children looked at him and looked at each other.

Chapter Four
The Amulet

W e don't know. The dwarf didn't give us any clue," said Sue. The children turned back around. Maybe the dwarf had forgotten to give them the clue, but he seemed to be busy doing exactly the same thing that he was doing when they got there.

"So what do we do now? We don't know what we're supposed to be looking for," said Sue.

At that very moment Mathew saw a stone that seemed to be glowing red. They hadn't noticed it when they went into the cave; it appeared to have some kind of writing on it. The children bent down and Mathew knocked off some dirt to see the stone better. It was covered in strange writing.

"The writing looks to be cryptic. Like ancient runes that early people used to use," said Mathew. Mathew and Sue had been home schooled by their father and had been taught of the ancient world so they were somewhat informed on some of the different hiero-glyphics that were used back in the day.

"Why don't we look in *The Book of Wisdom* and see if we can figure it out," Sue suggested.

Mathew and Sue sat on the ground and Mathew opened the book. The pages were yellowed and felt like old newspapers and crackled with each turn.

"Does it have any table of contents so that we could just turn to ancient runes?" asked Sue.

Mathew shook his head and continued to turn the pages slowly to avoid tearing them. As far as he could see, it was a complete manuscript on magic. The book began with a history of the earliest magic and then went on to describe the arts of working magic with herbs, crystals, and other magical objects, divination, and finally—what they were looking for—ancient runes.

"Here it is," said Mathew. He looked back at the writing on the stone. There were several different ancient runes recorded in the book. There were Egyptian, the Witches' Runes, German, and Scandinavian Runes to name a few.

"Let's see if we can match the symbols up so that we can decipher this clue," said Sue.

This was what was written on the stone:

μψ χολορ μεανσ
μψ λυχκψ νυμβερ ισ ονε
μψ φοοφ ισ ρεδ ανδ γρεεν
φινδ μψ φοοδ ανδ ψου ωιλλ φινδ με
ωηατ αμ ι

"Here, this one is closest to the symbols on the stone," said Mathew.

They looked closely and matched up the runes as best they could with the English letters that were in the book. And when they finished, it read.

A B C D E F G H I J K L M N O P Q R S T U V W X Y Z
α β χ δ ε φ γ η ι φ κ λ μ ν ο π θ ρ σ τ υ ϖ ω ξ ψ ζ

MY COLOR MEANS PURE
μψ χολορ μεανσ πυρε

MY LUCKY NUMBER IS ONE
μψ λυχκψ νυμβερ ισ ονε

MY FOOD IS RED AND GREEN
μψ φοδδ ισ ρεδ ανδ γρεεν

FIND MY FOOD AND YOU WILL FIND ME
φινδ μψ φοοδ ανδ ψου ωιλλ φινδ με

WHAT AM I
ωηατ αμ ι

"What do you think it means?" asked Sue.

Mathew continued to flip through the book, looking for anything and everything that could help them to solve the riddle.

"There's got to be clues in this book so that we can solve the riddle," answered Mathew.

Sue looked up at Sir Wilfred. "What do you think?" she asked.

"I am not allowed to help you. I am only here to take you to the places that you need to go," answered Sir Wilfred.

"Here's something," said Mathew, "It says here that the color white is for protection, peace, and purification. So I guess white means pure."

"That's great!" said Sue, "Now all we need to do is find something that's white and that has one of something."

"How do you know that it has 'one' of? It doesn't say that," said Mathew.

"Well what else could it mean? Lucky would mean that it was lucky for them, and that they have one. Maybe other things like them have more than one. Maybe that 'one' makes them magical, or maybe other things like them have none. It could go either way you know," said Sue, confusing herself a little as she spoke.

Mathew looked up at Sir Wilfred, who just shrugged his shoulders. Mathew continued to flip through the pages of the book.

"What about this?" asked Mathew. "It says here that unicorns are often found beneath apple trees and that their foods are apples."

"Which are red and green!" exclaimed the children together.

Sue continued: "Unicorns are white, and they have one horn. That's it! You're brilliant!" said Sue, smiling at Mathew. Mathew blushed. "Thanks. So now we must find an orchard where apples are grown," said Mathew looking up at Sir Wilfred.

"I know of such a place," said Sir Wilfred, holding out his hands.

Once again the children took hold of Sir Wilfred's hands, and once again the earth opened up. They began spinning out of control. This time, it felt like they were tunneling through the ground, spiraling down somewhere deep and dark, but it was all over within a minute. They fell gently this time. Sue and Mathew brushed themselves off and looked around. They were in a Garden of Eden, in the middle of an orchard. It wasn't just an orchard; it was an apple orchard.

"Great, let's look around for a unicorn!" said Sue. "It shouldn't take too long."

"We don't even know what we're looking for when we find one," said Mathew. "What do we need from it?"

"Well, you have the book," said Sue.

So, once again Mathew sat on the ground and Sue sat beside him. They continued to flip through the book's pages without knowing what they were looking for.

"Let's just go!" said Sue. "I think we'll find out what we need when we find a unicorn."

They both got to their feet and had only walked a few yards when they spotted a pair of unicorns under an apple tree, munching on apples. The unicorns were brilliant: they were solid white including their shiny, long manes, which flowed down their necks. They had dark, ebony eyes and one single golden horn protruded from each of their foreheads. Their tails flowed with radiance. The children gasped.

"I never knew that they really existed," said Sue. "They're beautiful."

The unicorns looked up at them, but were not startled. They continued to munch on their apples. As the children continued to watch the unicorns, they noticed that the sun was reflecting something on one of them.

"Do you see that?" asked Mathew.

"Yeah, I do. I wonder if that's what we need to get from the unicorn?" asked Sue.

Sue and Mathew began to walk slowly toward the unicorns. They each bent down and picked up an apple and continued toward the unicorns. The unicorns began to step backward as the children approached. The children held out the apples to the unicorns, and, finally, the unicorn with the shiny object on its neck bent forward and took the apple from Mathew. Sue gave her apple to the other unicorn. The unicorns allowed Sue and Mathew to stroke them like horses.

"They sure are friendly," said Sue as she smiled and stroked the gentle creature.

"Yeah, this was much easier than I thought it would be," said Mathew.

Just at that moment something swooped down and grabbed the object that was around the neck of the unicorn. The creature turned in midair and hovered with the object dangling from its spindly fingers, of which it had only three. It had a very big and mischievous smile on its face and within seconds it flew off into the nearby woods. The tiny creature was very small, about seven inches in length, with wings of about the same size.

"What was that?" asked Sue.

"The forest is full of magical creatures," answered Sir Wilfred. "That looked like an elf fairy. They are very sly and mischievous little creatures.

"Where can we find where he went?" asked Mathew.

"*The Book of Wisdom* will provide any and all information that you need to get the amulet back," replied Sir Wilfred.

"Amulet? Is that what that was?" asked Mathew looking at Sir Wilfred. But Sir Wilfred did not answer, for he seemed not to have heard the question.

Mathew sat back on the ground and flipped through the book. Sue sat next to him as he scanned the pages.

"There are gnomes, trolls, giants, ogres, goblins, Cyclopes, ghosts, ghouls, dwarfs, hobgoblins, fairies, Pegasi, dragons, elves, and—finally—elf fairies," said Mathew. "It says here that they're known for their mischievous behavior, and that they like shiny objects such as treasure and jewels. I wonder if they would trade such an object for the amulet."

"But what do we have that we could trade?" asked Sue.

"You have earrings on don't you?" asked Mathew.

"Well yes, but they aren't that shiny," said Sue.

"But they're diamonds aren't they?" asked Mathew.

"Yes. So what?"

"Then we can shine them up," said Mathew.

Sue removed her earrings and handed them to Mathew, who began to rub them with his shirt.

"There, they're shiny now," Mathew said, satisfied. "Let's go!"

The children walked into the forest. As they walked, they saw this cottony, small object floating in the air. It seemed to stay ahead of them the whole time. When it got stuck in a tree, a warm brisk wind would blow it free. It started to climb farther and farther up into the treetops until they could only catch a glimpse of it. It didn't move anymore, for the winds had stopped.

"Do you think that we should follow that cottony thing up into the trees?" asked Mathew, pointing at the tree.

"Probably; it's been with us the whole time, and elf fairies probably live in the trees," answered Sue.

So with that, they started to climb one branch after the other, with Mathew leading the way and Sue following. Sir Wilfred stood at the bottom of the tree, awaiting their return. When they finally got there, the cottony object let go of the branch and disappeared into the thick forest. The children just looked at each other as if to say, *now what?*

They sat down on two big branches and looked at their surroundings. They noticed a big nest that was just above their heads. Mathew stood up and accidentally hit his head on the bottom of the nest; within seconds they were surrounded by several tiny elf fairies.

"Buzzzzzzzzzz! Buzzzzzzzzzzz! Buzzzzzzzzz!" screamed the elf fairies.

"I'm sorry, I can't understand anything you're saying," said Mathew, rubbing his head.

Mathew looked down and saw Sir Wilfred take out the stick that was in his overcoat and pointed it toward the tiny elf fairies. From the end of the stick came a blue colored energy, which touched the elf fairies. Their language slowed down enough for Mathew and Sue to understand it.

"What are you doing destroying our homes?" screeched one of the elf fairies in a very fast and high-pitched tone.

"I didn't destroy it! I just hit my head," said Mathew.

"You caused a lot of damage!" said the elf fairy.

"I'll fix it, okay?" said Mathew.

"Why are you up here bothering us anyway?" asked another elf fairy.

"You took something of ours, and we need it back!" Sue responded sternly.

"What do you mean we took something of yours?"

"It was something one of the unicorns was wearing. When we were about to take it, one of you came and snatched it up," answered Sue.

"What did it look like?" asked another elf fairy.

"It was an amulet," said Mathew. "It was on a gold chain and the amulet looked like it was made of gold. It was very shiny."

"It was probably Hank. He has a collection, you know," said the elf fairy, smiling.

"So, how can we find this Hank?" asked Sue.

"I'll send for him," said the elf fairy, with a screeching whistle.

Within seconds, Hank was hovering in front of them.

"Whatcha need boss?" asked the tiny elf fairy.

"Did you happen to take a gold necklace from a unicorn?"

"Yes, that was the latest jewel to my collection," answered Hank, grinning from ear to ear.

"Well, we want it back!" demanded Sue.

"It's not yours!" screamed Hank, noticing them for the first time. The elf fairies wings fluttered so fast they looked as though they didn't move. Its' face was small and thin, so thin that it looked as though the skin was stretched over bone. Its eyes were big and round. Its legs and feet looked like those of chickens and its ears were very long and pointy.

"Well, we need it in order to save the wolf," said Mathew.

"Do you mean Quasar?" asked the first elf fairy.

"Yes!"

"Quasar has been dead a long time," said Hank.

"No! He's not dead; he's only half-dead. He's been turned into half a statue. He can't move, but he can still talk. We've talked to him. In fact, we're on a mission to gather objects in order to release the wolf from this dreadful prison, and we need the amulet that you have," pleaded Sue.

"How do you know that this is what you need?" asked the first elf.

"The wolf has sent us to find the items and all the clues led us to the unicorns. That has to be what we need," said Mathew.

"If this will help bring the Great Wolf back to us, then we need to give them the amulet," said the first elf fairy to Hank.

"We're willing to trade!" said Mathew excitedly, as he reached in his pocket and pulled out the diamond earrings.

Hank flew over to Mathew to get a better look.

"Those are nice and shiny, but are they real diamonds?" asked Hank.

"Yes, they are!" said Sue.

"I guess that's a fair trade," said Hank. He vanished for a split second and then returned with the amulet dangling from his spindly fingers.

"If this will bring the wolf back to us, it's well worth the trade. We owe a lot to the Great Wolf. Things used to be better than they are now," said the first elf fairy. "We are also imprisoned here in the forest. We are only allowed to go as far as the lake. Elf fairies who are caught beyond the lake disappear. Only heaven knows what happens to them."

The children thanked the elf fairies and started back down the tree. As they looked around they could see many nests in the treetops.

"We're lucky to have found the right elf fairy," Mathew observed to Sue.

When they arrived back on the ground, Sir Wilfred was still there. The children sat down at the bottom of the tree.

"We should look and see what we have," said Mathew.

Sue and Mathew dug in their pockets and pulled out an amethyst crystal, a piece of puzzle, and the amulet. They set down *The*

Book of Wisdom. Mathew picked up the amulet and started to look at it.

"I wonder if this thing opens up?" asked Mathew.

It looked as though there was a triangle on the amulet, though it was hard to make out. He set the amulet down and picked up the piece of puzzle. He noticed that the piece of puzzle was in the shape of a triangle, and that it also had a rune on it, which looked like: θ.

"Let's get the book out and see what letter it is," said Mathew.

"It's the letter Q," said Sue as she closed the book.

Mathew set the piece of puzzle down and picked up the amulet.

"I'm sure this thing opens up somehow. We need another clue," said Mathew, who was fiddling with the amulet and becoming frustrated. "Why doesn't this thing open up!?" yelled Mathew in total disgust. Then he hit the amulet on a nearby rock.

"What's wrong with you?" yelled Sue, scrambling away from him.

"It's this whole stupid thing! I'm sick of this whole stupid task that we somehow got stuck with! We don't know what we're doing and why we're the ones that have to do this. I'm hungry, tired, and I just want to go home!" and with that said, Mathew slammed the amulet down as hard as he could on the ground.

"Mathew, stop it!" Sue gasped. "You're scaring me. I know you're upset, but you have to keep going. I'm sure we're close to getting this whole thing figured out," Sue said, looking up to Sir Wilfred. He looked down at the children, silently, seemingly unfazed by Mathew's outburst.

"Are we out of time yet?" asked Sue looking up at Sir Wilfred.

Sir Wilfred looked at his time piece. "We still have ten hours."

"Ten hours!" said the children.

"It's been longer than that, hasn't it?" asked Sue.

"No," said Sir Wilfred. "I do have some more jerky if you'd like some."

"Yes, we would, thank you," said Sue, "and something to drink too."

Sir Wilfred once again pulled out a black pouch. He opened it up and pulled out three big pieces of jerky. He handed one to Sue, one to Mathew, and kept the third for himself. Once he returned the pouch to the inside of his jacket, he reached inside the other side of his shirt and pulled out a flask. He passed it to Sue, who took a couple of drinks and passed it to Mathew, who also took a couple of drinks and passed it back to Sir Wilfred. The children ate and drank until it was gone.

Mathew picked the amulet back up and looked at it again.

"I just don't know where to go from here," said Mathew. "We have no more clues."

"I wish that Quasar would have given us more information," said Sue.

Mathew gasped and dropped the amulet.

"What's wrong now?" asked Sue, looking at Mathew.

"Look!" said Mathew, pointing at the amulet.

They both looked down. The amulet had opened.

"How'd you do that?" asked Sue.

"I don't know. It was moving in my hands, and I just dropped it," said Mathew.

He picked up the amulet and pulled it apart the rest of the way.

"Look, there's another piece of puzzle and another riddle," said Mathew.

"What does it say?"

Mathew read:

My length is twenty-one inches long.
I make things happen.
The best ones can be found where the unicorns are.
What am I?

Sue picked up the piece of puzzle, which had a rune on it. She then looked through *The Book of Wisdom* and found the rune, which looked like this: ʊ.

"Well, we now have a U to go along with our Q," said Sue.

"Give me the book and I'll see if I can find out what this riddle means," said Mathew.

Mathew flipped through the old text to see if he could find anything that would lead them to their next clue. He saw a list of magical tools.

"Here it is. There is the knife, the cord, the sword, the bell, and the wand," said Mathew.

"So which one is twenty-one inches long?" asked Sue.

"Well it says that the knife is of any length that suits, and the same goes for the sword. Cords are nine feet long; bells of course, have no length, and the wand can be twenty-one inches long, or as long as your fingertips to the crook of your arm."

"We have to make a wand?" asked Sue.

"Yeah, and we have to go back to where the unicorns are," said Mathew looking up at Sir Wilfred.

Chapter Five
The Wand

Sir Wilfred held out his hands, and once again they went down into the earth, but this time it was very quick. It seemed that no sooner than they went down, they came back up. They were back in the orchard again.

Mathew sat back down and flipped the book open to the section on tools.

"It says here that the wand should be made out of, apple wood which is used for longevity. That must be why Quasar needs the apple wood wand," said Mathew.

Just then the amulet, which was in Mathew's pocket, closed shut. Mathew gasped.

"What's wrong?" asked Sue.

Mathew reached inside his shirt pocket and pulled out the closed amulet.

"It just closed in my shirt," said Mathew.

"I wonder what makes it open and close?" asked Sue

"Well it seems to open and close when we talk. Maybe a certain word that we say makes it open and close," said Mathew.

"What were we talking about?" asked Sue.

"I was just saying that Quasar ..."

And just then the amulet began to open.

"That's it!" screamed the two children. "It's Quasar!" And the amulet closed shut once more.

"That's interesting," said Mathew as he put the amulet back in his shirt pocket and closed *The Book of Wisdom*. The children stood up and began to walk over to an apple tree. Mathew took out a knife from his pants pocket and began to cut off a limb.

"Wait!" yelled Sue.

"What is it?" asked Mathew.

"It said in *The Book of Wisdom* that you have to ask permission before cutting a limb from a tree," said Sue.

"When did you read that?" asked Mathew.

"I've been flipping through the book off and on, and I remember reading that," said Sue.

"Who do you ask for permission?" asked Mathew.

"Whoever you're going to cut."

"Do you mean the tree?" asked Mathew, looking confused.

"Well, yeah," said Sue, who gave Mathew a dumbfounded look.

Mathew looked up at the tree and said, "May I cut a piece of limb from your branches?"

"What do you need it for?" came back a strong, deep voice in reply.

"Who said that?" asked Mathew, looking around.

"Whom did you ask?" came back the voice.

"I asked this apple tree," said Mathew.

"Then it is I," the voice responded once more.

"I need a wand made from apple wood to take to the Great Wolf. It will help return his power."

"Well, why didn't you say so? Anything to help the Great Wolf! I remember when he roamed these parts with his family. They were wild and free," said the voice. "Things were better then than they are now. We had more forests then. Now they cut and burn us without permission. They make things from us. We can no longer provide shade to cool the Earth as we once did when we thrived in these parts. We are becoming scarce. Do what you need to do so that we can once again become powerful in our own way. You have my blessing."

"Thank you, Sir," said Mathew.

Mathew began to cut the limb from a branch of the tree. Then he measured it from his fingertips to the crook of his arm.

"Mathew, it distinctively says twenty-one inches," Sue reminded Mathew.

"I don't have anything to measure it with. The book says either way will work."

"I hope you're right," said Sue looking worried.

Mathew stuck the limb in his back pocket, then looked at Sue and asked, "Now what?"

Sue opened up the book to wands, but couldn't find anything to help them. They were stumped. Sue then flipped the pages to spells, looking for anything that could be of use. She read something that could possibly help them later, but there was nothing to help them now. Just as she turned the page, something slithered across her foot. Sue screamed, scaring Mathew half to death.

"What is it?" yelled Mathew.

"I don't know! Something just scurried across my shoe. It looked like a snake!" said Sue.

"Look, there it is!" Sue said, pointing at it.

They took off running at the creature as they saw it go into a hole in the ground. They stopped when they reached the hole, and, to their amazement, the tail stuck out of the ground, wagging.

"Grab it!" yelled Mathew.

"You grab it!"

Mathew reached down and pulled the tail, but it wasn't a snake at all. In fact, it was a plant with roots, and a piece of puzzle and a riddle dangled from it.

"That was a snake, wasn't it?" asked Mathew.

"Well, yeah it was, but how could it just turn into a plant like that?" asked Sue.

Mathew shrugged his shoulders and grabbed the puzzle piece and the riddle. He handed the puzzle piece to Sue and he read the riddle. Sue flipped open the book.

The puzzle looked like this: σ.

"The puzzle is an S," said Sue. She closed the book and put the puzzle piece into her pocket. "What does the riddle say?"

Mathew read the riddle:

"I am the color of the life force that runs in your veins.
I am as long as the perennial magic number.
To make me, you will need the aid of cave dwellers,
for if sunlight shines upon them,
stones they will become;
entwine the words of a mute, the eyes of a stone,
the sweat of a pig, the beard of a child,
and the fire of a dragon.
Make me, and you will see the power that is within."

The children stared at each other with confused looks on their faces.

"That's really weird," Sue said, as she picked the book back up. "We still don't know what this root thing is." Sue looked up magical herbs, and she picked up the root that Mathew had laid down. She started to compare the root to other roots that were drawn in the book.

"Mathew, do you remember studying folklore when Father home schooled us?" asked Sue.

"Yeah, why?" asked Mathew.

"Do you remember learning that early herbalists or medicine men would name herbs after their appearance in nature?"

"Oh, yeah," replied Mathew.

"Well, it was a snake first, and then it changed into a plant with roots."

"Snakeroot!" they said in unison.

Sue quickly turned the page to snakeroot. "Here it is!" she continued. "The root is used to break hexes and curses."

"Great!" said Mathew as he stuffed the root in his pants pocket.

Just then the children looked back at Sir Wilfred, who was looking around nervously. The children walked over to him.

"What's wrong?" asked Sue.

"I don't know. Something doesn't feel right," Sir Wilfred replied. "Take hold of my arm." Sir Wilfred held out his arm and the children took hold. In his other hand he held the same object that he used to heal Sue's foot, which, Mathew and Sue realized, was a wand.

Chapter Six

The Surprise

This time, instead of going underground, they seemed to fly upwards. Their feet were off the ground, dangling. The children looked up and saw that a massive beast with large talons was holding onto Sir Wilfred. They were above the trees now, so high that birds were flying right next to them. They saw beautiful sapphire-blue lakes and white rushing water came from a babbling brook. Olive green grass surrounded the mesmerizing lakes, and skyscraping emerald green pines shaded the icy cold water. They also saw a mountain that seemed to be getting closer—too close for comfort. It looked as though they were going to crash right into it when the large beast dropped them into the mountain, which seemed to have opened up just for them.

Sir Wilfred got to his feet and brushed himself off. The children stood up and looked around. It was cold, wet, dark, and smelled, to their surprise, clean and pure. They couldn't see very far into the cave.

"Where are we?" Sue asked Sir Wilfred.

"We are in a cave where the witch has no power. We will be safe here," said Sir Wilfred.

"We can't stay here! We're running out of time!" said Mathew.

"We will not be here long. Just long enough to throw the witch off," said Sir Wilfred.

The children looked around. It was pitch-black. They couldn't see to far into the cave, but they could see a faint light in the distance. As they continued to watch the light, it seemed to be getting brighter and closer. They could make out a shape of a person carrying what looked to be a lantern. The person kept coming. The children began to get nervous. They drew closer to Sir Wilfred, who had a slight smirk on his face. Mathew could now see the person clearly. She was a beautiful woman: she was very tall, thin, and had long dark hair that went down to her ankles. Her skin was very light in color and her eyes sparkled like blue crystals. Her nose was straight and narrow and her cheeks wore a warm radiance. Her dress was of the royal color purple and was made out of lace, which flowed with elegance. The dress reached the floor, and her feet were adorned by shiny golden sandals.

"Hello, my children," said the woman, whose voice was very nice and soft.

"Hello," said Sue and Mathew.

"It is nice to see you, Sir Wilfred," said the woman.

"And you," said Sir Wilfred, who bowed and then walked over to her and kissed her hand.

"Things are moving along quite nicely, I suspect?" asked the woman.

"Yes, but there seems to be a disturbance in the energy field. Do you feel it?" asked Sir Wilfred.

"Yes, it is quite alarming," said the woman.

"Ahem! Excuse us," said Mathew, turning to Sir Wilfred. "Would you mind explaining to us what just happened here? We were brought here, or should I say, thrown here, by this strange beast, and now," he said, turning toward the woman, "there's you. Who are you?"

"I told you what happened," Sir Wilfred said. "The witch has felt the wolf become stronger with each object that you collect. I had to summon Nuri to bring you here for your protection. Nuri," Sir Wilfred explained, responding to Mathew's quizzical look, "is a dragon."

"A dragon!" exclaimed the children.

"Yes, and he is on our side. We interrupted his dinner, and what he caught got away. He was very hungry, so he had to go and hunt for something else," said Sir Wilfred. "That's why he slung us into the cave so quickly."

"And who are you?" Sue asked the woman.

"I am your mother," said the woman with a smile.

"Our mother!" screamed the children.

"Our mother is dead!" said Mathew scornfully.

"Is that what your father told you?" asked the woman.

"Well, no. He never told us what happened to her, only that she was gone. We just assumed she was dead," said Mathew.

"He's always known I was still alive. He can still feel my energies."

"What are these energies that you and Sir Wilfred are talking about?" asked Sue.

"The energies that surround us. The energies are everywhere: the trees, the plants, the rocks, the water, and the energies that run through us. We use these energies for positive change. This is what we call magic," said the woman.

"How do we know you're our mother?" asked Sue.

"I know your names. You are Mathew, and you are Sue," said the woman, smiling at each of them.

"And what is your name?" asked Sue.

"My name is Sylvia."

"That was our mother's name," said Sue looking at Mathew.

"Are you really our mother?" asked Sue hopefully.

"I would not lie to you, my children," said the woman, looking very sincere.

"Where have you been?" asked Mathew.

"We've missed you so much," said Sue, with tears in her eyes.

"I had no choice. The revolutionists were killing all of the royals; they were taking over. I had to find refuge. We had to separate, and we, meaning your father and I, thought it would be wisest for him to take you both into hiding. The wolf had already been taken, and that just left me. Nuri took me, and I've been here ever since," said the woman. "We all knew that it would happen one day. The wolf had put a spell in this mountain to protect it from the witch.

"How did you know that the witch would betray you?" asked Mathew.

"The witch kept asking the Great Wolf for different treasures so that she could perform magic for herself. The Great Wolf explained to her that he couldn't simply take anything that he needed unless he asked the royals first, and that they in turn would ask him what he was going to do with it. The witch became very angry and threatened the Great Wolf and the royal family. It was then that the Great Wolf took precautions and placed a protective spell over this mountain."

Suddenly, out of nowhere, Nuri the dragon was in the cave. He was as black as midnight with large batlike wings, which had hooks on top of them. He had a long snout with ridges and golden eyes that sparkled. There were two long, pointy horns on top of his head, with one shorter horn in the middle. His tail was long and scaly, as was his body, and his claws were large, sharp talons.

"Everything alright?" the dragon asked Sir Wilfred.

"Yes! I was a little startled earlier, but I'm better now. Thank you," said Sir Wilfred.

"He talks?" exclaimed Mathew.

"Obviously!" said Nuri.

"Amazing," said Sue as she walked toward Nuri.

"Can I touch you?" Sue asked the dragon.

"Yes, but sometimes I bite. I just can't resist fresh meat," said Nuri smiling.

She quickly pulled her hand back in fright.

"I'm just kidding. I really can't resist the opportunity for humor," said Nuri.

"A real joker," said Sir Wilfred.

"Yes, but a real lifesaver as well," said Sylvia, smiling.

Nuri smiled and showed his big white, massive fangs.

"Well let's not get all mushy about this," said Mathew. "We need to get going. We still need two more objects to gather for the wolf.

"Yes, we must go," said Sir Wilfred.

"What do you have?" Sylvia asked the children.

Mathew and Sue put their hands in their pockets and pulled out three puzzle pieces, and the amethyst crystal. Mathew grabbed at his pants pocket and pulled out the snakeroot and the amulet and then reached at his back pocket and pulled out the apple wood. He laid them out on the floor of the cave.

Sylvia picked up the puzzle pieces and started to fit them together. Just then Sir Wilfred grabbed her hand.

"We are not allowed to help them, or the spell will be unable to be broken," said Sir Wilfred, as he pulled back his hand and bowed down and said, "I am sorry Your Majesty, please forgive me. I was out of place."

"You are right, Sir Wilfred," said Sylvia, "but we are so close to returning power to the Great Wolf. You have nothing to be sorry for; I just lost myself in the excitement." Sylvia put the pieces back down on the floor of the cave and looked at the children. "Sir Wilfred is right, I cannot help you, but you are almost there. Once you have all the pieces of the puzzle, you must then fit them together and something wondrous will happen. You must now go."

The children put everything back into their pockets and stood up.

"The last riddle we have says that we must find the cave dwellers, for if the sun shines upon them, stones they will become. We must find who the cave dwellers are," said Mathew to Sue. Sue then picked up *The Book of Wisdom* and started to flip through the descriptions of magical creatures. She finally came to trolls.

"It says here that trolls will turn into stone if caught in sunlight."

"The trolls are in a place that is highly guarded by magic that I cannot penetrate," said Sir Wilfred. "Therefore Nuri will be the one to take you there. Are you ready for the journey?" Sir Wilfred asked Nuri.

"Yes," said Nuri, as he bowed his head in order for Sir Wilfred to pat the top of it.

The children walked over to Sylvia and hugged her.

"Will we see you again?" asked Sue, with tears in her eyes.

"Yes, we are very close now. We will be together once the Great Wolf is restored," said Sylvia.

"What about father? Will he be with us too?" asked Sue worriedly.

"Yes, we will be a family again," said Sylvia, holding her children tightly.

"Now you must go," said Sir Wilfred to the children. "Nuri will take good care of you, and you can ride on top this time." He picked Sue up and put her on top of Nuri.

Sue threw her arms around Nuri and held on tight, for she was scared of falling off. As for Mathew, he didn't need any help; he climbed right on up using Nuri as a ladder.

"It will only be the beginning once the spell has been broken. The revolutionists are still in control, and they will not be willing to give up their strong hold easily. There will be a war, but this time we will be ready," said Sir Wilfred. And with that said, Sir Wilfred smacked Nuri on the buttocks and Nuri raced out of the cave, but not before Sir Wilfred threw something around Nuri's neck. The children gasped and slung their arms tight around Nuri, although Mathew could not reach Nuri's neck; he hung onto Sue for dear life.

Chapter Seven
The Cord

They flew higher than before. They were high above the trees and mountaintops, soaring like an eagle. Mathew knew that Sue did not like heights and was worried that she was frightened. He could feel her tremble as he held on tight.

Everything was so beautiful. The mountains were of a musty gray and looked so rugged and steep. They were topped with snowy white caps; two billy goats were making their way up to the top, trying to avoid the two mountain lions that were trailing not far behind them. The maple leaves were a stunning golden color that shined like the hot sun, and the scarlet red oaks were as bright and brilliant as rubies. The contrast of browns and greens made the individual colors seem brighter. They saw the beauty of nature like never before. *This was the life*, thought Mathew.

They were not in the air long when Nuri started downward. Of course, Mathew could not tell where Nuri was going, but he did see a mountain that had a face on it. Not any face, but a face that looked like what he thought a troll might look like. It had one large eye that was opened and the other was covered up with brush and trees. The nose was very large, and the mouth looked as though it was opening. The children were getting very close now; in fact they were going into the mouth.

Once they entered the cave, the trolls seemed to scatter. The trolls disappeared into crevices, and some tried to hide behind one another. The cave was enormous, larger than the dwarfs'. It was wide open, without any scaffolding or machinery. There was a wide circle that was sunk into the ground and what looked to be an altar erected on it. The altar was decorated with gourds, pumpkins, and squash; golden colors radiated from it. One troll came out from hiding and said, "Nuri, it's only." The other trolls came out. They were very odd-looking creatures. They resembled moles; they had very large noses, hands, feet, and bellies. They had very long black hair, dark beady eyes, short stubby legs, and elongated bodies. There were men, women, and children.

"Nuri, here you brings what? Been it's time long. Assist we may how?" asked the troll.

"The children have a riddle that they have to solve which involves the help of trolls," said Nuri.

"Yes, we do," said Mathew as he slid off of Nuri. He immediately dug into his pocket and pulled out the riddle and read:

I am the color of the life force that runs in your veins.
I am as long as the perennial magic number.
To make me, you will need the aid of cave dwellers,
for if sunlight shines upon them,
stones they will become;
entwine the words of a mute, the eyes of a stone,
the sweat of a pig, the beard of a child,
and the fire of a dragon.

Make me, and you will see the power that is within."

"My, oh!" said the troll, as he walked back and stood by what seemed to be his mate. "Magic of kind worked not have years of hundreds." The troll squeezed and wringed his hands as if he would get something out of them.

"But you will be able to help us, won't you?" asked Sue worriedly.

"Everything gather to time much need but done be can," said the troll, now holding hands with his mate.

"How much time?" asked Mathew. "We don't have a whole lot of time. In fact, time is running out," said Mathew as he walked over to the troll.

"Read you riddle. Exist stuff do not. Talk don't mutes, eyes have don't stones, sweat don't pigs, and beards have don't children. Time much takes exist don't that things," said the troll looking at his mate for help.

"We understand that," said Sue, not quite understanding. "But we are on a tight schedule, and it was made very clear to us that we do not have a lot of time to spare, so if you could get started, it would be much appreciated."

The troll seemed to have understood Sue. At that very moment the troll walked over to the other trolls and they all huddled around him, including all of the women and children. Everyone seemed necessary. The troll in the middle of the circle began to point feverishly in every direction, giving each troll an assignment. As each troll received one, off they raced out of the cave. The sun had just dipped below the horizon, so they had no fear of being turned into stone. They had several hours of the evening to gather everything that was needed.

After every troll was gone, the troll looked back at the children and said, "Do must you magic of part."

"What do you mean our part?" asked Mathew looking at Sue and back at the troll.

"Must you cord provide, items the gather trolls," said the troll.

"What cord?" asked Sue.

"Said read you that riddle the, '*I am the color of the life force that runs in your veins. I am as long as the perennial magic number.*' Magic entwine trolls, cord provide must children," said the troll.

"We don't know how to make a cord," said Mathew looking at Sue.

"Riddles other getting been how?" asked the troll.

"Well, we've been using *The Book of Wisdom*," said Sue.

"It is where?" asked the troll.

"I have it!" said Nuri. "Sir Wilfred stuck it in a satchel and threw it around my neck just before he slapped me on my rump. It still stings."

"It have let's," said the troll as he walked over to Nuri, holding out his large hand.

"I believe that the children need to retrieve it, don't they?" asked Nuri.

"Right are you, believe I, yes" said the troll looking around at the children.

Mathew walked over to Nuri and took the satchel off of him and opened it up and took out the book and gave it to Sue. Sue found a section on cords.

"It says here that the perennial number is nine, and I'm assuming that the color would be red, for it's the color of blood which runs through our veins. It also says here that the cord needs to be of a natural substance, such as wool, cotton, or silk and three parts of the substance need to be woven into one."

"What about your shirt?" Mathew asked, looking at Sue.

"What about it?"

"What's it made of?" he asked.

"I don't know? What's your shirt made of?" Sue asked as if to make Mathew feel as awkward as she did.

Mathew walked behind her and pulled at the tag on her shirt. "Silk. That's a natural substance, isn't it?" asked Mathew to the troll.

"Yes, red not is it", said the troll, "Tag say your shirt?" he asked Mathew.

"I don't know."

Sue pulled at the tag on Mathew's shirt. "It says 100 percent cotton!" Sue exclaimed.

Mathew grabbed at his shirt and pulled it off. It happened to be the color red.

"Now what do we do?" asked Mathew, holding his shirt.

"Now we have to make it into three parts and braid it into one. Plus, we need to make sure that it's nine feet long," replied Sue.

Just then, the other trolls returned to the cave. The head troll walked over to the other trolls and asked, "We need, have everything?"

"Yes! Cord have you do?" asked the other troll.

"Yes!" replied the other.

"Perform magic we will," the troll said as he walked over to Mathew and Sue. "Braiding not starts till shirt torn sections of three. Begin you braid must materials as magic release trolls. Woven into cord as you braid, therefore unity created cord within;

done this will be energies filled. None lose ends knot tie. Understand you do?"

The children nodded their heads and began to rip and tear the shirt into strips using their teeth. When there was nothing left, the children reached down and picked up the pieces and walked over to the troll.

"Is this good enough?" asked Mathew.

"Perfect, yes!" said the troll. "Magic released, until braiding not start. Understand you do?"

Both of the children nodded their heads.

"Just tell us when we should start," said Mathew.

The troll walked over to Nuri and said, "This involved are you. Singed ends rope after ends are tied. Untied if knots come, seal the magic it will." Nuri nodded, and with that the troll walked to the middle of the cave. "Braiding the cord you will, once magic begins. Signal to you, will I," said the troll. The children held pieces of the torn shirt, waiting to begin.

The head troll stood at the altar, and the other trolls stood inside the circle and surrounded him. Nuri and the children also stood inside the circle. The trolls began to chant and sing, but they were singing in a different language. The children couldn't understand it, though they didn't mind. The less they knew, the better, they thought. The singing and chanting grew louder and louder, and then the trolls started to move. The one big circle turned into two circles; the trolls in the outer circle moved in one direction, and the inner circle moved in the opposite direction. The energies began to flow as the trolls divided into more and more circles, each moving in the opposite direction of the circle immediately outside of it. Soon the children saw something rise from within the circle.

It looked like a cloud, but within the cloud, they saw something that looked like a person, trying to talk.

"That must be the mute," Mathew whispered to Sue. Just then, the troll looked over at the children and nodded his head. The children began to braid as fast as they could when suddenly they felt an electrified jolt. Sue and Mathew looked up at one another. It startled them, but they did not let go of the material. They continued to braid even faster now. When they looked up, they saw another image above the trolls: the face of a troll inside a rock formation. The eyes were blinking uncontrollably inside the rock, and the children felt another jolt from the material. The children looked again at each other, but continued to braid. The next image was of a pig with water running off of him; his whole body dripped with sweat. When Sue and Mathew felt the third jolt, he was gone. Next out of the cloud came a child, who looked about seven years old. He had a full-fledged beard. With the next jolt, he was gone. The children were finishing the braid, and then each one grabbed an end of the cord. Before they could knot the ends, out popped what looked like a puzzle piece from each end, and something else—maybe another riddle. All of the objects hit the floor of the cave. Then the children knotted each end of the cord and turned to Nuri, who added the finishing touches. He singed both ends with his fiery breath.

The trolls rushed to the children with excitement, for it had been such a long time since they had performed such an extraordinary task.

"Cord the measure must we. Long feet nine be must it," said the troll.

"But we have no way to measure the cord," said Sue.

"Measure with Boulder we will. Nine feet tall exactly he is. Of all the trolls, the biggest he is," said the troll. "Boulder!"

Boulder stepped forward. He was huge. He looked exactly as the other trolls, but he was double their size.

"Assistance my need you do, Slate?" asked the giant troll.

"Cord the measure to need we, yes. Long feet nine be must it. Around turn you could?"

Boulder turned around, and the children handed the cord to Slate. The whole cave was disturbingly silent. Slate motioned for two other trolls to stand behind Boulder. One climbed on top of the other and reached down for the cord. He held the cord to the top of Boulder's head and the cord dangled down, just barely touching the floor. It was no longer silent. Once again the trolls began to clap, cheer, sing, and dance. Sue and Mathew looked at each other and smiled; they, too, began to laugh and dance.

After they were out of breath and could dance no more, Sue picked up the two puzzle pieces and the riddle that came out of the cord. Sue handed the riddle to Mathew and Sue looked in *The Book of Wisdom* to translate the runes on the puzzle pieces. The two pieces looked like this: α, ρ.

"We now have an A and an R!" exclaimed Sue.

Mathew read:

> Fit all the pieces of puzzle together, and
> it shall spell out the servant and the master.
> This shall be what is needed to bring about precious change
> and to restore the power to the Great One,
> For with this cord you shall imprison,
> for all of eternity,
> the evil that has caused great harm
> to everyone and to everything.

"Puzzle of pieces the all have you do?" Slate asked the children.

"No, we don't. I think we're still missing one, aren't we?" Mathew asked Sue.

"We now have five pieces of puzzle. I think we need six to be able to fit them all together," replied Sue

"Amulet you have?" asked Slate.

"Yes," said Mathew. He pulled out the amulet and handed it to Slate.

Slate took the amulet from Mathew and said, "Surname is what?"

"Robert," said both children together.

The amulet, which Slate held in the palm of his hand, opened up and produced another puzzle piece, which looked like this: α. Sue took the puzzle piece and feverishly flipped through the pages of *The Book of Wisdom*. "It's another A."

"The puzzle of pieces triangle they form, match up they must to the top of *Book of Wisdom*," said Slate.

The children gathered all the pieces of the puzzle and fit them together. Mathew saw that the pieces of puzzle spelled out Quasar on one side, and on the other it spelled out the name Robert. The puzzle made a triangle, which fit perfectly into the faded triangle on the cover of *The Book of Wisdom*. When Mathew fit the triangle into place, the whole cave began to spin out of control, including the trolls, Nuri, and the children. It was like the whirlwind of a tornado. The children tried to hold onto one another and to speak, but no one could hear anything. The trolls had expected something because they had all huddled together: the male trolls surrounded the women and children. They were tightly bound together with their strong hands.

Nuri tried to maintain his composure by flapping his wings and hovering. He couldn't stop himself from bouncing into the trolls, but this did not break the magic that held the trolls together.

The tornado did not move in any direction, and it only lasted a few minutes. Suddenly, everything stopped and Mathew and Sue were once again in the forest. To their amazement, they were looking once again at the Great Wolf.

Chapter Eight
The Breaking of the Spell

Quasar looked different than before. There were signs of fur on the dead half of his body, but he still had no eyeball and he could not move. He was also not alone. There were people, wolves, and other creatures in the forest. The unicorns, the elf fairies, the trolls, the dwarfs were all there as well as other creatures the children had never seen. Nuri, Sylvia, and Sir Wilfred were near the wolf as well.

"Hurry children; we have all been waiting. Do you have all of the objects with you?" asked Sylvia.

"Yes, we have everything," replied Mathew. Mathew and Sue placed each object on the ground by Quasar's feet. The objects were the amethyst crystal, the amulet, the snakeroot, and the apple wood.

"Well done children," said Quasar. "Now comes the easy part. When we begin the magic, the witch and all her counterparts will arrive, but we will be ready for them. Do you have the cord?"

"Yes, it's right here," said Sue, holding up the cord.

"You will use the cord to cage and imprison Kai, the wolf who is my brother. I did not have time before, to speak of him. You must now know the whole story," said Quasar. "When the revolutionists came, they went to the witch and threatened to harm me and the royals if she did not bring them gold, silver, and precious jewels. When the witch asked me for the jewels, I refused because I thought she wanted the treasure to satisfy her own greed. The revolutionists then turned to my brother Kai, who, without my knowledge, had turned against me. They promised him my place if he betrayed me and a chance to rule the new kingdom. They told him that he would receive the credit for building the best kingdom in history. He, in turn, put pressure on me and the royal family into supplying the revolutionists. In which, we did not. He threatened that the witch would kill the royal family and destroy the kingdom. He told us that the witch had become evil, and that she wasn't going to let anyone stand in her way. He was reinforcing that the witch was bad. The witch and I had worked closely together before, when we performed healing magic for the royal child. We had worked close enough for her to know my strengths and weaknesses."

"It was not long before I discovered Kai's betrayal and the witch came to act as his emissary. She told me of the spell that she and I had actually worked on long before the revolt actually happened if we should ever need it. She perfected it and told me that it could be broken once the children became of age. I did take precautions and had another spell put into place that if something should happen to me things could then be restored. I agreed to the plan and let her take me deep into the forest, where no one could find me. It was then that she put this terrible spell on me, but in reality, she saved my life. It's true," Quasar said, in response to the grunts of disbelief and indignation from the crowd around him.

"She knew that I would be tortured, and later killed, when I would not provide the revolutionists with precious jewels. She also knew that the royal children would some day be of age to take back the royal kingdom and break the spell. The witch went to Sir Wilfred and told him her story, and that it was now time to take back the kingdom; the royal children were now of age. She explained to Sir Wilfred that the royal children could now break the spell, but that they only had twenty-four hours to do it, and we haven't much time left. Once the spell is broken," Quasar said, addressing Sue and Mathew, "take the cord about a hundred yards away from me and construct a cage. It is a magic cord, and it will grow when you pull it, and it will lock when you jerk it to the side. You must shape the cord into a cage with four sides. It will be bound with magic, so once Kai is inside he will not be able to get out. In other words, we are setting a trap for him. Do you understand?" asked Quasar finally, his voice deepening.

There was urgency and anticipation in the crowd that could be felt as the air was stagnant and the wind was silent. There were many whispers and discussusions coming from the audience as the suspence rose that was felt as worrisome but also excitement, for they had waited ten long years for this nightmare to end.

"Well, you haven't told us how to break the spell," said Sue.

"It will happen in much the same way as you made the cord. Everyone will gather around and form a circle; we will be in the middle. You will construct the wand with everything that you have gathered: the quartz crystal, the amulet, the snakeroot, and the apple wood. You also need something else from the unicorns in order to attach the quartz crystal to the apple wood. Once you have discovered how to do this, you will need to insert pieces of the snakeroot into each end of the amulet. Once this is done, you will repeat these words as you move along with the others in the circle:"

'We must chant, sing, and dance around
in order to break the spell.
Once the spell has begun, you will hear the sound.
We have the power; there is no room to fail.
We must continue in order to restore the crown.
If we cannot do this, then you will hear us wail.
We must continue the chant in order to release the hound,
and ensure that Kai is forever jailed,
and with the cord be forever bound.'

"We must continue the chant until the spell releases me, and all power is then restored," said Quasar.

"What do we do with the wand and the amulet?" asked Sue.

"Once you have constructed the wand, as I have described, then you must insert the wand into the amulet. You may have noticed the quartz crystal is in the shape of a triangle; it will fit inside the triangle on the amulet. When you push the crystal into the amulet, it will release a force that will help me to regain strength and power. You mustn't do this until I give you the signal. In order to unlock this power, we must have already raised enough power by chanting and dancing. When these two powers meet, the spell will break," said Quasar.

"This may sound difficult, but once the spell is broken, it will turn into pandemonium. I will go after Kai and chase him toward you: you must have the cage ready. Most of the pack will be here, then. Some of them will be on our side, and some will fight for him. The revolutionists are human. There will also be some creatures on Kai's side. It will be interesting to see who will stay with him," mused Quasar. "If there are no further questions, we must get started."

"Yes, I am ready for this to end," said Sue, who had been silent, taking it all in.

"Yes, I too am ready for this to come to an end. Hopefully it will all be worth it," said Mathew.

While they were talking, the forest had begun to fill with humans, wolves, twice as many trolls, elf fairies, dwarfs, unicorns, and other creatures that they had never seen. The creatures had begun to form a large circle around the Great Wolf and the children. There were several hundred, and still more were coming. Sir Wilfred and Sylvia greeted each and every one of them. They seemed excited to finally put an end to this evil magic.

The children asked the unicorns who had gathered what else they needed from them. The unicorns bowed down in front of the children. The children looked at each other and smiled.

"I bet we need hairs from the unicorns to attach the crystal to the apple wood," said Sue.

"I think you're right," said Mathew smiling. Mathew and Sue began to gather the hairs from the unicorns. The hairs were very strong, and silvery in color. Once they had the hairs, they began to wrap the quartz crystal onto the apple wood. Mathew took out the knife that he always carried in his pocket and began to cut pieces of the snakeroot. Sue had the amulet in her hands and said, "Quasar." One side of the amulet opened. Mathew inserted pieces of the snakeroot and said, "Quasar." The amulet closed. Sue turned the amulet over and said, "Robert." The amulet opened. Mathew inserted snakeroot and said, "Robert." The amulet closed once again. They had finally constructed the wand.

"We are now ready," they told Quasar, and showed him the wand.

"Gather round everyone, for it is time," said Quasar. "The moon is full and bright, and full of energies. We must use them wisely." While Quasar was talking, still more people and creatures joined the circle. "Come join the circle," he told them, in a loud voice, "so that we can combine the energies that we have to restore the power of the crown and The Great Wolf."

As he spoke, the circle began to move. The crowd seemed to be mumbling something, but it was too faint to hear. The children were also in the circle; Mathew held the wand, and Sue held the amulet as they moved with the flow of the crowd. The chant began to grow louder. As more and more people and creatures joined the circle, it became larger. When the wolf saw that the number of people, animals, and creatures coming into the circle had begun to dwindle, the wolf said, "Now the circle is closed; we have enough. We can now use our energies to restore our power."

The chanting grew even louder now, and the circle moved faster. The people, animals, and creatures seemed to become more enthusiastic and more anxious as the circle began to fill with more and more energies.

From the circle rose a gray cloud: the energies began seeping into the air. There was no laughing or smiling in the circle, only solemn faces. The energies began to increase, and the color of the cloud began to change from gray to blue, and from blue to black. Mathew felt as though he could almost reach out and touch the cloud, for it was so thick and solid. From the cloud came a strong smell of fire and ash, and heat. The cloud was now a deep red.

The chanting was even louder than before, and the circle moved faster; they were almost jogging. There came a brisk wind, and the cloud began racing around in circles, almost like a tornado spinning out of control. The leaves on the trees began to whistle.

The children could just barely see the wolf, for now the cloud was very thick and foggy. The wolf gave what looked like a nod to the children. Sue and Mathew looked at each other; Sue held out the amulet and Mathew thrust the wand into it. The amulet flew out of Sue's hand and went racing into the wind. From the amulet, colorful sparks shot out in every direction: blues, reds, greens, purples, yellows, and even some colors that were unidentifiable. The circle filled with these energies, which seemed to be shooting in everyone's direction.

The wind also changed; it began to move in the opposite direction, and it was even faster than before. There was debris in the wind: leaves, rocks, and dirt. The wolf began to change: he was no longer on the ground. In fact, he was in the air. He was floating and spinning with the cloud. His legs moved as though he was running. He stayed in the air until the winds finally died down, and then he reached the ground slowly. The clouds disappeared as fast as they had appeared. The colors were no longer there; the chanting stopped, and the circle became still. The wolf stood majestically in the center of the circle. The amulet and wand lay on the ground, at the wolf's feet.

Chapter Nine
The Cave

The Great Wolf was brilliant; there was a golden glow of radiance that flowed from him. He was fully intact, with two big bright blue-crystal eyes, a full gray fur coat, a long snout, a long bushy tail, and elongated ears. Everyone gazed at him in awe.

Sir Wilfred and Sylvia rushed toward him, but there was little time to celebrate, for Kai the wolf came out of nowhere and pounced upon Quasar. The powerful energies of the two wolves threw Sir Wilfred and Sylvia backward. The wolves went at each other growling, snarling, and biting. The animals and creatures were totally taken by surprise. The circle spread out and eventually collapsed to where some were seeking protection under the trees.

The mighty wolves were rolling on the ground, as each was fighting to keep the other down. Each pierced his long canines into the other's hard, thick skin. It was not long before blood flowed on both coats, though it was not possible to know whose blood was whose. Kai grabbed Quasar with his massive fangs and threw him into the centaurs, nearly causing a domino effect. Quasar quickly got to his feet and ran at Kai, butting him in the head. Kai flew into the air and immediately fell to the ground. Quasar ran at him, probably to finish him off, but Kai grabbed him once more and locked his jaws and massive canines into Quasar's snout, pulling Quasar to the ground. Quasar lay on the ground whimpering and whining; he stopped fighting back.

Kai let him go and addressed the silent audience, "Here is your so-called all-powerful Great Wolf! He is pathetic! Look at him! He has never been all-powerful! I am your King! I have always been greater than Quasar, and now I have proved it!" Kai spat in Quasar's face and pounced on him. Kai began parading back and forth turning his back on Quasar looking on and addressing his audience. The audience began backing up even further into the woods. Some even seemed scared for their lives. Kai's coat was darker than Quasar's-—it was almost black and not as full. His eyes were a deep brown and his ears seemed to droop.

"He has been defeated once again, and this time he will not return!" As Kai's back was turned, this time addressing the two children, Quasar rose to his feet. The pulsing energies that surrounded Quasar were a deep, dark red. Quasar ran at Kai and hit him with enough force literally knocking Kai deep into the forest. Kai was gone. Quasar raced off to find him.

As Quasar predicted, chaos broke loose. While the two wolves fought deep in the forest, the other creatures were also fighting. The good trolls were fighting the bad trolls—they all swung their fat clubs at one another, crushing heads. Soon, trolls littered the ground. Boulder was even there, but he didn't need a club for his giant arm and hand seemed to work just fine. He bashed the trolls and other rogue fighters into the ground. The good unicorns were fighting the bad unicorns; they used their golden horns as swords.

Sylvia and Sir Wilfred were also fighting the revolutionists. The revolutionists seemed to be coming from everywhere. Sir Wilfred swung his wand back and forth—it emitted a blue stream of energy that knocked the revolutionists to the ground. The ground opened up and swallowed the bodies. Sylvia had a sword that was small, but powerful. When she swung her sword, it emitted a purple energy that was even more powerful than Sir Wilfred's. When she struck the revolutionists with her sword, they flew up into the trees, and the trees wrapped their limbs around them, holding them captive.

As the fighting continued, Sue and Mathew plunged into the woods, about one hundred yards away from the circle, out of sight from the fighting as the wolf had instructed them. They worked together to construct Kai's prison with the cord. They pulled and jerked the cord to make a cage big enough to hold Kai. Suddenly, they looked up and found themselves surrounded by centaurs. The centaurs each had the head and torso of a man, which rose from the chest and shoulders of a horse. Not knowing whether they were good or bad, Mathew and Sue both stood in front of the prison as if to protect it.

"What do you want?" asked Mathew.

"What are you doing?" the largest centaur responded, who was the closest to the children and the other centaurs continued to encroach into the childrens space. "We are not allowed to say." said Sue.

"Is that for Master Kai?" asked the Centaur.

"It is none of your concern," said Mathew.

"It is our concern if it is meant to hurt our Master," replied the centaur.

"It will not hurt him, for it is only a prison to hold him," replied Sue.

"Don't tell them anymore! They don't need to know anything!" shrieked Mathew.

The centaurs moved closer to the children, so close that the children backed all the way up to the cord. There was nowhere else to go. Mathew and Sue looked at each other for they had not been prepared for anything to go wrong. The centaurs were massive in size and very intimidating. The children were very scared and they had nothing to fight with. The largest centaur nudged Mathew hard in the stomach with his nose. Mathew grabbed his stomach and wobbled a little bit, almost falling into the prison. Just then, a big wind swept through the trees, and a large shadow covered the ground.

"Nuri!" the children yelled.

Nuri blew fire at the centaurs, and they scattered.

"They'll be back," Nuri told them. "But now, I have something for you." Nuri motioned to his back and said, "Those are for you. They are to help protect you in case someone or something tries to harm you again. Take them."

Mathew grabbed the objects. It was a scabbard, and it contained a golden sword. He quickly attached it to his belt. He then grabbed the other object, which was a bow and a quiver full of silver arrows. He handed the bow and quiver to Sue, who swung them around her shoulder.

"Thanks Nuri! We didn't know what to do when those centaurs cornered us," said Mathew.

"I must now go. The revolutionists have sent for the dragons from the West, which are known for their brutality. I must try to prevent them from coming here. Master Mathew and Lady Sue, I wish you success," Nuri said as he bowed down to the royal children.

Both Sue and Mathew hugged Nuri, then off he went, up through the trees, and he was soon out of sight.

The children quickly returned to the cord to finish making the prison. They continued pulling and jerking the cord to make it big enough for Kai. Once they had finished, they joined the fight. They felt more confident now that they had weapons.

Quasar and Kai were gone, but Sir Wilfred and Silvia were still going strong. Sir Wilfred was still swinging and thrashing his wand, knocking the revolutionists to the ground with its blue light. Sylvia continued to swing her sword with all her might, knocking the revolutionists into the trees, which held them captive. Mathew had his sword out waiting for action and Sue had an arrow loaded in her bow ready to fire at any moment.

Just then, a wolf landed on top of Mathew and knocked his sword to the ground. The wolf was feverishly biting at Mathew's face. Mathew was trying desperately to push the wolf off of him, but to no avail. He used his arm to search for his sword and used his other hand to protect himself from the wolf. He was struggling; he felt pain in his face, something warm and wet streaming down his cheeks. He knew he would be dead in a matter of minutes if he couldn't find his sword. Suddenly, the wolf went limp and Mathew pushed him off. Mathew looked up, and there was Sue with the bow in her hand and no arrow. He looked over at the wolf and saw an arrow protruding from its back. Sue pulled Mathew up and threw her arms around him.

"I almost lost you!" Sue exclaimed, with tears rolling down her face.

"Thanks, I thought I almost lost me, too. What took you so long?" Mathew asked to make Sue laugh. "We had better get back to the cage; we weren't really supposed to leave it. We were supposed to wait for Quasar to chase Kai into it. I hope we didn't miss him." Mathew grabbed Sue by the arm and ran back into the forest.

"It's gone!" Sue gasped. "Where do you think it could be? This is where we left it, isn't it?" Sue and Mathew were desperately running back and forth, searching for the cage.

"I can't believe that we messed up!" shouted Mathew. "We both forgot to stay with the cage." Mathew grabbed his head with his hands. "We've got to find it!"

"Look!" said Sue, who pointed up the hill. They could see what looked like the cage. When they found it, they could see that it was not like they had left it. It looked as though something had dragged it. They grabbed hold of it and brought it back to its original spot. Once again, they began to pull and jerk the cord to finish the cage. Once finished, they did not move from it again. They waited for the wolves, and resisted the temptation to join the fight. Mathew's face burned a little from the scratches that he now had because of the attack of the wolf, but lucky for him it was just scratches. It could have been worse.

They could hear violent noises and confusion coming from where the fighting was taking place. They also felt something rumbling through the trees, and it seemed to be getting closer to them. It sounded like someone or something was running frantically through the trees. The children looked very hard in that direction and within minutes they saw something run right into the cage. They had caught something! It was a wolf! It was Kai! Quasar stood directly in front of them.

From out of the forest came a woman who the children did not know. She had very pale skin, long, dark red hair, a very slender build, and a full face with a long, narrow nose. She was wearing a red dress that went down to her bare feet.

"Seal the cage, Xaviera!" yelled Quasar to the woman. The woman held up a wand and shot a reddish stream of electricity toward the cage. In an instant, a lock appeared on the cage. Kai raced back and forth, trying to break through the invisible force field that held him.

"Where were you?" asked Quasar, gently to the children.

"We're sorry" said Mathew. "After we put the cage together we thought that we should help fight. I was almost killed by a wolf that attacked me. If it wasn't for Sue, I'd be dead right now," he said, taking Sue's hand.

"What happened to the cage?" asked Sue to Quasar. "We put it together, but when we came back, it was gone."

"I chased Kai into the cage but it was not stable without your presence. He dragged it up the hill, and then he escaped. I needed Xaviera to seal it and lock it into place. It is invisible to Kai, which is how we caught him again," said Quasar.

"You are the royal children?" asked the redheaded woman.

"Yes, I am Mathew and this is my sister, Sue," said Mathew.

"Are you the witch?" asked Sue.

"Yes, I am the witch, Xaviera," said the woman in a calm, soft voice.

"I don't mean to be rude, but shouldn't we get back to the fight?" asked Mathew, looking at Quasar.

"Yes, we should, but most of Kai's followers know that he is restrained, and have already fled. Yet a few will stay and fight to the end. We must go," said Quasar.

Sue and Mathew followed Quasar and Xaviera to the battle. They saw that Sir Wilfred and Sylvia were still fighting. Several of the revolutionists were restrained by the trees. They saw a man fighting very close to Sir Wilfred and Sylvia. He didn't have a wand, but was fighting very exuberantly with a golden sword. Before they had a chance to look more closely, they joined the fight.

Mathew had his sword out and Sue was ready to take aim with her bow and arrow. Soon, several revolutionists swarmed them. He and Sue were surrounded. Mathew started to swing his sword with all his strength. Sue pulled back her bow and launched an arrow. The arrow pierced one of the revolutionists, and he immediately fell. Sue pulled out another arrow from her quiver, and another arrow went flying. It struck another revolutionist. Mathew swung his sword, and he slashed an enemy in the shoulder. The man fell to the ground, screaming in agony. As Sue and Mathew continued to fight, the revolutionists fell one by one. *This isn't that hard at all*, thought Mathew.

As the fight continued, Sir Wilfred, Sylvia, and the unknown man joined Sue and Mathew. Mathew looked over at Sue, who was fighting off a centaur who had knocked her to the ground. She was in trouble and could not pull back her bow. Mathew tried to rush over to her, but the unknown man beat him to it. Mathew watched as the unknown man plunged his luxurious sword into the centaur. The centaur fell and the man reached down and pulled Sue up onto her feet.

He thought he heard Sue say "Father?"

Mathew continued to fight. Several gnomes had sought him out. They were no bigger than a foot and a half tall, and only came up to his knees. They had pointy red hats and their pointy, long ears stuck out along side. They had big, black feet that were way too big for their bodies, and large bellies. They looked as though they liked to eat. Mathew immediately began kicking at them, and they went flying. Some soared into the air and hit the revolutionists, knocking them out cold. Some sailed into trees, and the trees restrained them. Mathew called Sue's name, and when she looked over, he yelled, "Catch!" and kicked a gnome her way. Sue caught the gnome and threw it at the centaur she was fighting. The gnome grabbed on to the back of the centaur and the centaur rode off with the gnome on its back. Once the centaur rode away, the other rogue fighters also left.

Sue and Mathew looked around, and to their amazement they were surrounded by Quasar, Sylvia, Sir Wilfred, the witch Xaviera, and their father, William.

"Father!" screamed the children. Sue and Mathew ran to their father. They were so happy to see him. They had not known whether they would ever see him again, let alone find him fighting by their side. They both grabbed and hugged him.

Their father was a tall, handsome man in his mid-forties. He had thick, wavy, dark brown hair, brown eyes, and his skin was golden brown.

"Does this mean that we're going to be a family again?" asked Sue looking at her father.

"Yes it does," said her father, looking at Sylvia with a smile and a sparkle in his eye. "Yes it does," said Sylvia, who walked over to them. She gave both the children a hug and a kiss, and then reached her hand to William, and he took hold.

"This is not over," said Quasar, looking at the happy family. "They will be back with reinforcements. We will be able to catch our breath, but that's all. Sir Wilfred, have you seen Nuri?"

"No, I have not," said Sir Wilfred.

"We saw him," said Mathew. "He saved us from some angry centaurs. He said they would be back."

"Did he say where he was going?" asked Quasar to Mathew.

"He said that he had to go and head off the dragons from the West," said Mathew.

"The dragons from the West are brutal, and Nuri won't be able to fight them alone. Hopefully he went to gather the dragons from the East, South, and North to help him fight them off. We should also be prepared to fight the dragons; he'll need all the help that we can offer," said Quasar.

Soon the sky darkened, and large shadows covered the ground. The children ran to a clearing so they could see what was covering the sky.

"It's dragons!" yelled Mathew.

"Come, we must take cover," said Quasar.

Quasar started to run and the children, Sir Wilfred, Sylvia, and William followed. They quickly reached a nearby cave. Once in the cave, the children realized that they were missing someone.

"Where is Xaviera?" Sue asked.

"Xaviera will be fine, and so will you if you stay in the cave," said Quasar.

"What do you mean?" asked Mathew.

"What he means is that we must go to help Nuri, and you must promise us that you will stay here where you will be safe," said William.

"You can't leave us here! We must go and help fight! We're not afraid of any dragons!" said Mathew.

"You both have done exceptionally well. We could not have done any of this without you. Now let us handle the dragons. We cannot afford to lose either one of you now," said Quasar.

"That's why we need to come! You can't do this without us, you need us!" pleaded Sue.

"Children, if you want us to be a family again, you must do as you are told. This will make everyone safe. We will not have to worry about either one of you getting hurt if you both stay in the cave," said Sylvia.

"Master Quasar, we must go," said Sir Wilfred, looking at the Great Wolf.

"Yes, we must. Now children, do as you're told, and we will return for you when the fighting is over. Don't disappoint me again," said Quasar as he motioned for the others to follow.

William and Sylvia hugged the children before they started after Quasar and Sir Wilfred.

"I don't believe this!" said Sue. "After everything we've been through, they're going to make us stay in this cave and do nothing!"

"Who says that we have to stay here?" asked Mathew.

"You heard them! We have to stay here, so they won't have to worry about us." said Sue.

"We're kids! We don't always listen to adults, do we?" asked Mathew as he walked over to the mouth of the cave.

"What are you getting at?" asked Sue, who looked at him strangely.

"They're not here to babysit us. We can just walk out!" said Mathew.

"Maybe we should listen. You remember the last time we defied the wolf. You were almost killed," said Sue. A tear trickled down her face.

"Sue! Come on. After everything we've been through, how can we sit here and do nothing? I know you're scared; I am too, but they need us. If they didn't, Sir Wilfred wouldn't have come for us in the first place. Everything will be alright; you'll see," said Mathew as he grabbed Sue's hand.

As the children attempted to leave the cave, they walked into an invisible wall.

"What the devil was that?" asked Mathew.

"They must have sealed the cave with magic, to make sure that we wouldn't leave," said Sue.

"I don't believe it. They don't even trust us," said Mathew with a slight grin on his face. "Now what are we going to do?"

"We could just sit here, like they told us to do," said Sue as she sat down.

"We could go inside the cave. I'm sure that there's another entrance somewhere," said Mathew, as he began to walk toward the back of the cave.

Sue followed Mathew toward the back of the cave, and they made their way through the cave very slowly. The floor of the cave was very slick because of the water that had gathered, and the sides of the cave were cold and wet. The cave was very cool and brisk.

"Sue, are you alright?" asked Mathew. "It's so dark that I can't see you anymore."

"I'm just going slowly so I won't fall. It's so slippery," said Sue.

"What do you think lives in this cave?" asked Mathew.

"What do you mean? Do you think they would put us in a cave with something else in it?" asked Sue.

"Maybe they haven't been all the way through the cave," said Mathew.

"Mathew, are you trying to scare me? If you are, it's working," said Sue.

"I don't mean to scare you, but you should prepare yourself just in case," replied Mathew.

"Let's just change the subject. How do you think mother, father, and the others are doing?"

"I'm sure they're doing just fine. I'm not going to worry about them," said Mathew.

The children tried to find other things to talk about to keep their minds busy. They progressed very slowly. They slipped and fell on rocks, and small pebbles got into their shoes. Sue was cold, and since Mathew still had no shirt, he was freezing. He imagined himself in front of a warm, glowing fireplace wrapped in a wool blanket in their cozy cabin. Sue also imagined them back home in the cabin, but this time Mother would be with them.

The cave seemed to go on for eternity. They could not see any light, which would indicate a way out. Mathew worried that maybe Sue was right. Maybe they should have stayed put. He remembered the last time they had disobeyed and had done a great disservice to Quasar.

Sue screamed.

"What's wrong?"

"My foot slipped, but a rock or something kept me from falling any further," replied Sue.

As Sue regained her composure, she heard a groan that seemed to come from the rock that broke her fall.

"Did you hear that?" asked Sue.

"Hear what?"

All of a sudden, the entire cave lit up. A flame came from the rock near Sue's foot. Sue and Mathew screamed and then it became dark again.

"What was that?" asked Mathew, reaching for his sword. To his surprise, it was gone.

"Sue, pull out your bow and arrows!" yelled Mathew.

Sue reached for her bow, and discovered that it was gone as well, along with all her arrows.

Chapter Ten
Olaf

Who dares enter the lair of Olaf!" bellowed a deep, dark voice.

"It is I, Mathew, son of William and Sylvia."

"And I, Sue, daughter of William and Sylvia," said Sue.

The monster blew a flame, lighting torches that lined the perimeter of the cave.

The children could now see what had been talking to them. It was a dragon. He looked very similar to Nuri, only older. His skin was gray in color, wrinkled, and droopy. He had bags under his eyes and his teeth were black, broken, and rotten.

"So you are the famous royal children," said the dragon.

"Yes, I guess we are. And who are you?" asked Sue trying to act brave.

"I have already told you. I am Olaf, and this is my lair. Why have you come here to disturb me?"

"It is not our fault. The Great Wolf, Quasar brought us here and told us to stay, but we're trying to find a way out," said Mathew.

"Why do you defy the mighty wolf, Quasar? There are not many who would do that, unless you are his enemy," said Olaf, looking suspiciously at the children.

"We are not his enemies; in fact we are the ones who broke the curse. We want to help him and the others to fight off the dragons from the West," said Sue.

"What did you say? The dragons from the West?"

"Yes, the dragons from the West. Do you know of them?" asked Mathew.

"We fought them many years before, and we were almost destroyed. They did us great harm. That was many years ago. Who accompanies the Great Wolf in this mighty battle?" asked Olaf.

"There's our father and mother, William and Sylvia, along with Sir Wilfred and the witch, Xaviera. Oh, and of course, Nuri," said Sue.

"Xaviera? She is the one who cursed the wolf. Why would she be helping in the battle?" asked Olaf.

"She put the spell on the wolf so that we, the royal children, could break the spell and then take back the royal kingdom," Mathew explained.

"Did you say Nuri was with them?" asked Olaf.

"Yes, do you know him?" asked Sue.

"He is my son," said Olaf.

"Your son!" exclaimed the children.

"Yes, didn't you notice the resemblance?" Olaf smiled and showed his rotten teeth. "We are both very distinguished."

The kids looked at each other and giggled.

"Why are you in this cave?" asked Sue

"I live here!" said Olaf.

"So, did Quasar know that this was your cave?" asked Mathew.

"It's been a long time, but I'm sure he remembers," said Olaf. "Why do you ask?"

"We don't know why he put us in this cave," said Mathew.

"You did say that the dragons from the West were coming, didn't you?" asked Olaf.

The children nodded.

"You are needed to take back the royal kingdom. Quasar cannot take a chance that something might happen to you. So as they said, you will be safe here," said Olaf.

"But we can help fight! We've done it before! We helped to fight off the revolutionists, the centaurs, and lots of other creatures!" shrieked Sue.

"These are the dragons from the West; they are barbaric. They are the meanest and foulest creatures on the face of the Earth. They do not play. They will destroy anything and everything that gets in their way. They do not give up, nor can they be reasoned with," explained Olaf.

"But you and Nuri are dragons, and you are not like that. You seem to be rather nice," said Sue smiling.

"These dragons are from the West. They are not like other dragons. They have caused great harm throughout history. They have destroyed farm lands and farm animals, forests, dragons, and humans. They kill for no apparent reason. You do not want to be near when they are around," said Olaf, and he continued." It's been many years ago that the dragons from the West invaded Celestial City."

"What is Celestial City?" asked Sue.

"Celestial City is the name of the Royal Kingdom in which you both will rule. These parts in which we stand are part of the Royal Kingdom. They took us by surprise. We were not prepared for war. They killed my mate, Nura, Nuri's mother. They eat their kill. They tried to take her body, but they were unsuccessful. She is buried on top of this mountain, where we lived. She is honored by all other dragons. She died by protecting the eggs of dragons and the many chicks that were only days old. Nuri and his brother were there when they attacked. Nuri's brother was also killed in the attack," Olaf's voice cracked and he looked down and finally he said, "We were unable to retrieve his body. Most of the eggs and chicks were saved. Nuri was able to kill the dragons that were there when other dragons came to help. They killed so many of our kind that we were nearly wiped out. That is why Quasar put you here. For your protection," Olaf put his head down. "Quasar helped us to defeat the dragons from the West. This was many years before the revolt."

The children walked over to Olaf and put their arms around his neck and Sue and Mathew stroked his rough skin. "I'm so sorry Olaf," said Sue. "I'm sorry that you lost your mate and your son. If you don't mind me asking, what was his name?"

"Odin, his name was Odin; my first born," said Olaf. Things became quiet for several minutes.

"Olaf, what kind of dragons are you and Nuri? You talk about the dragons from the North, South, East and West. That is all the dragons from each direction, but what are you called?" asked Mathew.

"We are Spirit dragons. We are called that because most everything lives through us. If we all die then most everything that is good will die. That was another reason I was hiding in my cave. As long as one lives most everything that is good has a chance to survive. Did you notice that you had no weapons when you entered my lair? No one can bring weapons into my lair, not even you. Quasar made it so."

In order to cheer things up a bit Olaf told them about the old days when Sylvia was a young girl in the forest. "She rode on Quasar's back, just like a pony, through the forest, and she played with all the wolf cubs in the pack. Those were the good old days," said Olaf.

"Do you mean that our mother, Sylvia, was the royal child that Quasar was to keep healthy and well?" asked Sue.

"Yes. Didn't you know that?" asked Olaf.

"No! No one has ever told us that," said Mathew.

"Quasar and Sylvia became very close. Whenever you would see Quasar, Sylvia wouldn't be too far behind," said Olaf.

The children noticed a round object in the center of the cave, where Olaf was standing. They hadn't noticed it before, but now it glowed a deep red and radiated heat. Sue was trying not to look at it, but it attracted her attention.

"What's that?" Sue finally asked, pointing to the object.

"That is an orb," replied Olaf.

"What does it do?" asked Mathew.

"An orb gives off light and heat, but it is also an object used in divination," said Olaf, gazing into the orb.

"How does it work?" asked Mathew. He was drawn to the orb's light.

"The orb feels the energies that surround it, and it seems to know what you need from it. It tries to provide that need," said Olaf, trying to fight off the hold that the orb seemed to have on him.

"Can I touch it?" asked Mathew looking at Olaf.

"Yes, but please be careful. The orb will attach itself to the person or object that touches it, and it will not release easily," said Olaf. He seemed uncertain.

"Be careful," said Sue, looking very worried.

Mathew picked up the orb, and immediately his face felt as though it was shriveling up. His face thinned, his eyes bulged, and his ears turned red as fire.

"What's happening? Do something!" Sue yelled at Olaf.

"The orb is connecting with Mathew. It is scanning every part of his body. If it doesn't release soon, I will break the connection," said Olaf.

Mathew's cheekbones looked as though they would break out of his skin at any moment, and his skin stretched thinly over the bones. His nose grew very thin, and his eyes bulged out of his head, red blood vessels covering the whites of his eyes.

"Do something! It's killing him!" Sue yelled. Her face was as white as a sheet, and she was trembling all over. She was watching Mathew die right in front of her.

Olaf touched the orb with his wing and immediately the orb's energy was drawn toward the dragon. It soon released Mathew, and his face returned to normal.

"That was incredible!" said Mathew, who could not tear his eyes from the orb. "We really connected!" He still seemed be drawn to the orb's energies. He was fighting to look away. Finally, he looked at Sue and saw the horrific look on her face.

"What's wrong?"

"What's wrong? You should have seen your face! It looked as though it could split at any moment! Your ears seemed to be on fire, your nose became almost nothing, and your eyes bulged out of your head, and you want to know what's wrong?" asked Sue who was still in shock.

"I felt a little strange, but it didn't hurt," said Mathew as he walked over and gave Sue a great big hug. "I'm okay."

Mathew looked over at Olaf, who placed the orb beside him. "So the orb was feeling me—like it was getting to know me?"

"Yes, the orb now knows you inside and out. It can help you answer any questions that you may have," Olaf said.

As Olaf, Mathew, and Sue gazed into the orb, it began to change colors. The colors turned from red to deep purple, to deep blue, to dark green, to bright yellow, and it finally settled on dark purple. Then, words appeared inside the orb.

"What's it doing?" asked Mathew.

"It's telling you what you want to know," said Olaf.

"But I didn't ask it anything."

"Well, it wants to tell you something, whether you asked it or not," said Olaf.

Mathew walked over to the orb.

"Mathew don't touch it!" Sue yelled.

"I won't," said Mathew, to ease her anxiety.

"It should be alright," said Olaf. "The orb knows you now. It will not grab hold of you like it did before."

Mathew bent down and picked up the orb. "I can't read it," said Mathew. He gave the orb to Olaf.

"It is in the language of the trolls. It's gibberish, meaning that it is all mixed up. Do you have *The Book of Wisdom* with you?" asked Olaf.

"No, we had it at one point, we seem to have lost it," said Sue.

"You will need *The Book of Wisdom* to decipher this message. You could also ask the trolls; they could decipher it. Do you know where you lost *The Book of Wisdom?*"

"Well, we had it when we broke Quasar's curse, didn't we?" asked Sue, looking at Mathew.

"I think so. We were in the forest," said Mathew.

"It would be to your advantage to know what the orb is telling you. It may help to end this war, once and for all," said Olaf.

"Will you come with us?" asked Sue.

"I have not left this cave in ten years—not since the war started. I thought this exile was something that I must accept. Things had changed for the worse, and there was nothing that could be done. You have given us hope again. Go and find *The Book of Wisdom* and bring it here. If you cannot find the trolls, I will try to help you decipher the orb's message."

The children grabbed hold of the old dragon and each kissed his rough, scaly face. "You may have to take the orb with you, for it possesses protective energies that you may need in order to return safely. This is the only way that I can allow you leave the cave without Quasar's permission," said Olaf, as he attempted to give the orb to Sue. Sue stepped back, terrified.

"Since you have the same purpose, the orb will need to know you both; therefore you must let the orb feel your energies so that it can protect you."

"I guess it looked worse than it felt," Mathew said. "It doesn't hurt; it just felt weird. You'll be all right, I promise."

Sue looked at Olaf, and she took the orb from him. The orb grabbed on to her as it had with Mathew. She started tingling all over, and she felt her entire body go numb. Sue could feel her face tightening, and her ears felt as though they were on fire. Her eyes seemed to be drawn into the orb; she saw things as though she were inside the orb. She could see Mathew and Olaf watching her. It was all red, then pink, then purple, then dark green, then bright yellow, then blue, and then back to a deep purple. She could see Mathew speak to Olaf, and she saw Olaf touch the orb to break the connection. The orb's energies were drawn out of her, and then it released her. She felt faint and dizzy, but she could feel Mathew's arm around, which kept her from falling.

"Are you alright?" asked Mathew, knowing now how Sue had felt watching him.

"That was strange," said Sue, still drawn to the orb, just as Mathew had been.

"Did it hurt?" asked Mathew.

"No, but I could feel my face and body being drawn, like yours was. My ears were hot, and I could see you both as though I were inside the orb," said Sue.

"You were inside the orb in a way," said Olaf. "Your body wasn't physically inside the orb, but mentally you were there. The orb has to bring you inside of it so that it can connect with your energies and know what you are feeling. That's its way of getting to know you."

"We still don't know our way out of here. Can you help us?" asked Mathew.

"Yes, the orb will light your way as you continue to go deeper inside the cave. You will see a light—walk toward the light and you'll come to a small opening. It will be just big enough to squeeze through. Remember to come back with *The Book of Wisdom* so that I can help to decipher the orb's message. Now, off you go until we meet again," said Olaf.

Sue and Mathew walked deeper inside the cave. Mathew thought they were better off now that they had the orb to light their path. Eventually they could see the light the dragon told them about. It was still far away, and it didn't look close to the ground. Mathew was not sure how they were going to be able to reach the exit. They made their way to the light and just as Mathew had thought, the exit was above the ground; they would have to climb to get out. Mathew looked around for something to step on in order to climb out. At that very moment, the orb started to change in Sue's hands. She screamed and Mathew turned to see what had happened. The orb that was in Sue's hand was no longer a small, round sphere. It had grown to the size of a boulder; Sue dropped it because it was heavy.

"Wow!" exclaimed Mathew. "What did you do?"

"I didn't do anything!" yelled Sue, who was gazing at the big rock.

"Didn't Olaf say that the orb would provide the need of the one who was holding it?" asked Mathew.

"I think that's what he said. We needed a rock or something to stand on, so now it's a boulder," said Sue.

Both children pushed the boulder below the exit.

"You go first," said Mathew to Sue.

Sue climbed on top of the boulder and pulled herself up to the hole. She was small enough to get through it, and climbed out. Mathew climbed out of the cave right behind her. "What about the orb?" asked Sue. "We can't leave it."

Mathew put his head back into the cave and saw that the orb was small again and glowed blue.

"Think about the orb," said Mathew. "It will know that we need it."

Sue and Mathew thought about the orb. The orb started to bounce on the floor of the cave; it bounced high enough for Mathew to grab it through the hole. It still glowed blue, and it held the message inside, which was written in the language of the trolls.

"I wonder what would happen if we thought about *The Book of Wisdom*. Will the orb show us how to get it back?" asked Mathew.

"I guess we could try," said Sue.

Both children thought about the book and gazed at the orb. The orb started to glow bright blue, then red, then green, then purple, then pink, then back to red, where it stayed. Inside the orb, they saw *The Book of Wisdom* lying on the floor of a cave, with trolls walking by.

"It's still in the troll cave, where we made the cord," said Sue.

"Perfect! We need the trolls' help to decipher the message. But Nuri took us there. It's way up on top of a mountain, and I'm sure that we couldn't possibly climb it by ourselves," said Mathew, looking bewildered.

"Let's use the orb again. Maybe if we ask how to get up to the troll cave, it will tell us," said Sue.

"Okay!" said Mathew.

Both children looked at the orb and asked together, "How can we get up to troll mountain?"

The orb started to glow again. This time it filled with fog and the children couldn't see anything. Clouds formed and spun around. Pictures started to appear inside the orb. First there was a dragon, which looked very similar to Nuri, then a Gryphon, an animal with the body of a lion and the head and wings of an eagle, then a Pegasus, a winged horse that was white as cotton. It stopped on this picture.

"Is that what we need to take us to the trolls?" Mathew asked Sue.

"You're asking the wrong person, silly. Why don't you ask the orb?"

Mathew looked at the orb and asked, "Is that what we need to take us to the troll cave?"

There was no response from the orb. There was only the image of the Pegasus. Apparently that's what the children needed in order to get to the cave, but where to begin?

The children sat by the orb, not knowing what to do. The message reappeared, and the orb was blue again. As the children sat there gazing into the orb, they heard something above the treetops. It was a noise that they had heard before, when Nuri had come to their aid against the centaurs. They ran to a clearing in the trees in order to see what it was. The children were in awe; it was a Pegasus, and it looked exactly like the image the orb showed them. Its body was cottony white, with huge white wings, a long white mane, and a long, flowing white tail. The children backed up in order to give the Pegasus plenty of room to land.

Once the Pegasus had touched ground, the children ran to it, but it startled the Pegasus, and he reared up. The children backed away, and Mathew grabbed Sue's hand. Once the Pegasus calmed down, the children once again approached the Pegasus, but this time with caution.

Sue and Mathew each had their hands out in front of them as they approached this beautiful creature. Once they got near enough, they began to stroke its long mane.

"I wonder if it will let us ride it to troll mountain," asked Sue.

"I'm sure that's why it is here. Obviously the orb sent it to take us there," said Mathew.

The Pegasus knelt down, inviting the children to mount it.

"You first," said Mathew, holding out his hand to give Sue a boost.

"Why, thank you, Sir," Sue said, as Mathew boosted her up onto the gentle creature.

Mathew grabbed a hold of the mane and then heaved his leg over the Pegasus, being careful not to do anything that would startle it.

Once mounted, the Pegasus took flight. The wings were huge as they flapped up and down. The Pegasus seemed much smoother than flying with Nuri for some reason, but Mathew figured it was because they had done this before, and they knew what to expect.

Mathew looked around, and saw something flying right next to them. It startled him at first, thinking it was something out to get him, but then realized it was only a bird. They saw rivers, lakes, and birds nesting in treetops, just as they had when they flew with Nuri. They saw herds of deer grazing in the meadows and rabbits scurrying in their holes. Further down the way, they saw wolves, lots of wolves. Large packs that seemed to be fighting and chasing one another. Could they have found Quasar? Mathew looked at Sue and then at the wolves. A little further down, they saw people who were also fighting. Were these the revolutionists? Seeing this, Mathew's thoughts immediately went to his mother and father. Are they down there fighting? Are they alright? Mathew could feel his face growing hotter by the minute; he was beginning to get angry. *Why did they make us stay in that cave, when we could be down there fighting alongside them right now?* He thought.

Mathew smelled smoke and looked in another direction. The smoke came from the trees up ahead. The forest was on fire. Then he saw the dragons, who must have caused the blaze. They were fighting: the dragons were blowing fire at each other, and were burning down the forest in the process.

One dragon whizzed past the children and the Pegasus, narrowly missing them. But another dragon in hot pursuit passed right in front of the Pegasus and clipped its wings. Suddenly, the Pegasus and the children were spiraling out of control.

"Hold on Sue, this could get ugly!" said Mathew as he tightened his grip on Sue and the Pegasus.

"Oh, my gosh, we're going to die!" replied Sue as she put her head down as though to pray, and she tightened her grip on the Pegasus.

Soon the whole sky was filled with nothing but dragons. They fell closer and closer to the ground. They really were going to die.

Mathew had put the orb in his lap between him and Sue to keep it from falling off. Mathew grabbed the orb and screamed, "We need help!"

The Pegasus was trying to overcome the obstacle, but somehow Mathew knew that the Pegasus's wing must be broken, and therefore it would have to land with just one wing. They needed to get off the Pegasus in order for it to survive.

The dragons zipped by left and right, closely following one another. Flames flew from their mouths. Mathew and Sue kept their heads down and covered them as best they could, which was difficult. They didn't know if they would survive. The ground continued to grow closer.

Then, somehow they were no longer on the Pegasus. The Pegasus was flying in front of them. It safely reached the ground in one piece. As for the children, giant talons lifted them. They were flying further up into the clouds where they could no longer see what was happening on the ground.

As they flew toward the mountains, Mathew recognized Troll Mountain, which looked like a troll: one eye was open and the other eye was covered with brush and trees. The nose was big and wide, and the mouth was open, and they were going in.

Chapter Eleven
Muth-Wella

It was like before; the trolls scattered as soon as they entered the cave. Then Slate, the head troll came out.

"Olaf, time long been. Troll Mountain, what brings here you?" and like before, Slate's mate came out and stood faithfully beside him, along with the other trolls.

The children turned around in awe. They knew that Olaf had not been out of his cave in many years and weren't sure if he could fly anymore.

"Yes, it's been a long time, Slate. The children have informed me about everything that has been happening since the war started. It seems the Great Wolf has returned to us, and it's time we took back our lives," said Olaf. "The children have an orb and inside of it is a riddle that is in troll language and needs to be translated so that they can solve it."

"Where's the orb?" asked Sue, looking at Mathew.

"I don't know. I had it, but I must have dropped it when Olaf grabbed us" replied Mathew.

"We must find it!" said Sue and she started for the cave entrance.

"Why?" asked Olaf.

"You just said we must find the orb in order to solve the riddle," said Mathew.

"No, what I said was that the riddle needed to be translated. I know the riddle, or, I should say, I memorized it," said Olaf.

"But you said that we needed the trolls to translate it for us," said Sue.

"I memorized the gibberish message, but the trolls will need to make sense of it," said Olaf.

"Message the is what?" asked Slate, looking at Olaf.

Olaf spoke:

> Oohlah goolah loolah kapala haalala naalah.
> Raaulah taguuau papalakaa Woorh plooh.
> Aaughlooh klaaupt toolauuw kauuta.
> Paoola Kuuala woorh plooh wuua taaugol.
> tuooltal guualot guooalrt wuualt.
> Puualgha luaapulrh woorth tuaalha koolap.
> Toolta koophla ruutoop gaaloh nooulk wootlh.
> Raaulah paaulh woorh plooh ooalkp aauplth.
> guuatlh gopoht paakgh uugtah pootgthp.
> Kaaltho taoolpt gooalt raalpt nuuaalgt.

"Make should this sense perfect. Talk you as reads it," said Slate. "Sense make should it so backwards reads it."

"That is why it confused me; I know that trolls speak backwards," said Olaf.

Slate translated:

In the mouth and well of the Serake Tribe lies the El Castrum Del Serpere Pluma. Give forth the rainbow eye to the serpere, and restore its vision. Once restored, the serpere will slither to the ground taking all serpere with him, leaving only the true master and those loyal to the throne.

"And what does that mean?" asked Sue.

"It means to say that lost eye has serpent plumed. Find it must you and it must you restore. War ends all for and once," said Slate.

"And how do we find the plumed serpent?" asked Mathew.

"'Muth-Wella' is a Serake word meaning mouth and well of the Serake Tribe," Olaf explained. "The most famous pyramid is the El Castrum Del Serpere Pluma, which means Castle of the Plumed Serpent. Legend has it that once you place the missing eye of the serpent on its statue, the serpent will slither down along the side of the northern staircase and take with it all the serpents, leaving only the true master and those loyal to the throne."

"Quasar mentioned that it would be interesting to know who was on his side and who was on Kai's. This will prove who is really loyal," said Mathew.

"How will we be able to get to Muth-Wella from here, and how will we be able to find the eye of the serpent?" asked Sue.

"I will take you," said Olaf. "As for the eye of the serpent, where did you lose the orb?"

"Is that the eye of the serpent?" Sue gasped.

"Well it could be," said Olaf. "The message did say something about the rainbow eye."

"Yes, and it changes to all the colors of the rainbow," said Mathew.

A noise came from the entrance of the cave. It sounded as if someone or something was entering. Mathew and Sue turned around to find another dragon in the cave; to their amazement, it was Nuri. He had something in his mouth and dropped it on the floor of the cave. "Did someone drop this?"

It was the orb! It glowed pink, then red, then blue, then black, and it stopped on purple.

"Where did you find it?" asked Mathew, as he walked over to Nuri.

"I saw it fall when Olaf grabbed you both. I had a dragon on my tail and had to blow him out of the sky before I could go after it," said Nuri, as he smiled and showed his white, massive fangs.

"How is the fight?" asked Olaf.

"We are doing well, but there's still no end in sight," said Nuri.

"How are mother, father, and Quasar?" asked Sue.

"Your mother is very strong-willed, just as you are," Nuri said looking at Sue. "Your father is a very good warrior," looking at Mathew. "Quasar is very determined to restore things as they once were. His pack is very loyal to him, but the others are very loyal to the revolution. Once Kai was captured, Quasar knew that it was only the beginning of the war."

"We must get to Muth-Wella to restore the serpents eye. This should bring peace," said Mathew.

"Yes, he is right. We must go," said Sue, looking at Olaf.

"I told them that I would take them to Muth-Wella to restore the eye," Olaf told Nuri.

"It's good to see you, Olaf, and we can use your help," said Nuri.

"It is good to see you, Nuri," said Olaf. "Now, come children. We must go."

The children climbed onto Olaf, Sue first, with Mathew behind her. Nuri picked up the orb with his large mouth and handed it to Mathew.

"Don't drop it this time," said Nuri.

"I won't."

And with that, Olaf and the children were once again out of the cave and flying just below the clouds. They were finally going to end this thing once and for all. They would be a family again, but this time mother would be with them.

Chapter Twelve

Quasar and the Eye of the Serpent

The sky and earth were littered with dragons. The scarlet red forest crackled and sizzled, and the smell of burning ash polluted the air. The smoke was so thick that it was hard to see things clearly. The children could see the revolutionists on the ground, running around and swinging their swords, slashing and stabbing anything and everything that got in their way.

Mathew spotted the pack of wolves that were fighting close to Quasar. He was amazed at just how much energy radiated from Quasar. He saw the red aura that flowed from the Great Wolf. Mathew remembered that red, according to *The Book of Wisdom*, meant strength and courage, which Quasar had in abundance, for he was truly a hero.

Mathew and Sue continued to watch the fight, which seemed to go on for miles. They saw their mother, father, and Sir Wilfred fighting the revolutionists. They watched as a man attacked their father. William stumbled and fell; he was in trouble. The man had his sword at William's throat, but then William reached for his sword, which was lying by his side, and ran it through the man's stomach. The man fell. Then they saw Sir Wilfred grab Sylvia by the hand and run with her, taking her away from the fight. Was he protecting her? Where were they going, and why were they leaving William and Quasar by themselves with all those revolutionists? Sue and Mathew lost track of Sylvia and Sir Wilfred; they were gone.

Mathew felt something warm on his back, like a furnace. He turned around and saw a dragon very close behind them. The dragon was blowing flames at Olaf.

"Olaf, we picked up a dragon!" said Mathew.

"I know, hang on!"

Olaf swerved violently, nearly knocking the children off his back. The dragon once again blew another flame and caught Mathew's hair on fire. Mathew swatted at his hair, trying to put out the fire. He could feel the singed hair at the ends. His back felt as if it were sunburned.

Olaf swerved the other way, zigzagging across the sky, but the dragon was still there, hot on their trail. The dragon seemed to know all of Olaf's moves. Olaf swerved again, but this time he seemed to make a complete circle, and they were no longer in front of the dragon, but behind him. Olaf blew a flame at the dragon: not just one, but several. In fact, Olaf kept blowing until the dragon's tail was in flames. The dragon and its wounded tail flew to the ground.

"Well, I've still got it!" said Olaf, as he smiled.

Finally they could no longer see the war, and the dragons were gone. The sky grew dark, for the sun was setting. Olaf was no longer flapping his wings; they seemed to be gliding through the air.

The wind began to blow harder; the sky darkened, and the clouds thickened.

The atmosphere was changing rapidly, and so were the mountain ranges. There were less mountains and more plateaus. They could see lots and lots of trees, so many trees that it started to look like a jungle, or a rain forest.

Though the sun previously appeared to be setting, it now appeared to be rising. Had they gone through some kind of portal? Had they left one world and entered another? Mathew and Sue could see old ruins made of stone, which looked like they had been built many centuries before. Pyramids were coming into view. One of the buildings looked as though it was an observatory, used for star exploration. Another looked like it was some kind of stadium, maybe used for sporting events.

Sue looked behind her at Mathew with an excited, but scared, look because at this point they were not too sure what to expect, only that they were ready for the fighting to end.

Olaf landed just outside the stadium-like building. Mathew and Sue dismounted. Mathew still had the orb that he had carried between his legs while riding Olaf. The orb no longer displayed the message, but it continued to turn from pink to red, from red to blue, from blue to black, and from black to purple. It was changing colors at an alarming rate, like it knew that something was going to happen. It grew hotter and hotter. Mathew took care not to drop or lose the orb again, for he knew that it would allow them to end the war and return home.

The air was very dry, but very hot. Olaf moved toward the pyramid.

"Stay close children; I feel we are not alone," said Olaf. "There's something very unsettling here."

The children ran to close the gap. Mathew too could feel something, but he did not know what it was. Of all the different places they had been, this was the strangest. The children had felt at home in the magical world, but this place was different. It possessed a different atmosphere, and it was much hotter than any of the other places they had been.

They were in an open field where they were easy prey. The children watched intently for any movements. The sky was clear with no clouds in sight, and the sun beat down without mercy.

They were almost to the big pyramid when the sky turned dark with dragons.

"Run!" shouted Olaf. Mathew grabbed Sue's hand and began to run as fast as he could. "Run to the pyramid," said Olaf. "I will try to hold them back!"

Mathew continued to run, holding onto Sue with one hand and holding the orb with the other. They finally made it to the pyramid and ran inside.

"Are you okay?" asked Mathew, panting.

"I'm pretty scared," answered Sue, who was shaking. "What about you, are you okay?" asked Sue.

"I'm alright," answered Mathew who was still trying to catch his breath. "Well, all we have to do now is find this serpent and return his eye. Then all of this will be over."

"Do you remember when Quasar told us that we could go home when we broke the spell that the witch had put on him? We're still here, Mathew. I don't think we'll ever be able to go home again," said Sue, as tears trickled down her face.

"Please Sue, don't lose hope now. Remember we have mother now, and we'll be a family again. Some good will come out of this, you'll see. It'll be over soon. I promise. First we need to find the serpent."

It was very dark as they continued to make their way further inside the pyramid. Mathew went first, and Sue followed, holding onto Mathew's belt loop. The passage ways were very narrow as they walked along the walls.

"Don't trip, Sue. There's a step right here, there's another one. We seem to be going downstairs," said Mathew.

The children kept going downstairs, but they still couldn't see anything. Things kept popping into Mathew's mind like, *What were they going to run into? Who were they going to run into?* Sue was really getting scared now, and Mathew knew it. He reached for her hand and he could feel her hand sweating and trembling.

"Are you okay?" asked Mathew.

"I'll be alright. Can you see anything yet?"

"Not yet, but I'm sure it won't be long now," said Mathew, without certainty.

"Mathew, during the battle, did you see father plunge his sword into a revolutionist who was going to hurt mother?" asked Sue.

"No I didn't see that," said Mathew.

"What did you see?" asked Sue.

"I'm not sure," said Mathew.

"What is that supposed to mean?" asked Sue.

"I saw something, but I'm not sure what it means."

"You're not making any sense."

"I know," said Mathew.

They continued to follow the wall of the pyramid, when suddenly the wall started to move; it opened up to another pathway. Mathew screamed, which scared Sue even more than she already was. Mathew squeezed Sue's hand to calm her down. He saw a faint light in the distance, through the new opening which was just what he needed to focus his eyes on. They continued to move slowly toward the light. They were still going down, but the steps were gone; they now seemed to be walking down a ramp that was very wet and slick.

"Be careful Sue," said Mathew, holding Sue's hand.

"Weren't kings buried inside these pyramids with their precious jewels?" asked Sue.

"Yes. Why do you ask?"

"I wonder who's buried in here."

"Don't worry. A lot of these pyramids have been looted, therefore nothing is left in them," said Mathew.

"What if they never found anything?" asked Sue.

"Don't be silly. It's been here a long time. I'm sure there's nothing left in here! Ahhhhh!" screamed Mathew and Sue.

The floor gave way, and the children went tumbling down a long shaft. They traveled at a very high speed down the shaft before coming to an abrupt halt.

"Are you hurt?" asked Mathew, with his heart in his throat.

"Ow! I am now. The orb just hit me in the head," said Sue as she rubbed her head. "Now where are we?"

"I'm assuming that we're still in the pyramid," said Mathew, looking around.

"Do you see anything?" asked Sue.

"You know what? We forgot that we have the orb. We could use it to light our way like we did before," said Mathew.

"You're a genius, Mathew. I forgot about it too," said Sue.

Sue picked up the orb and said, "Light our way," and at that very moment the orb shined a very bright light.

"Wow! That's bright!" said Mathew. "Now maybe we'll be able to find our way out of here."

As the children turned around to go back to where they had come, they could now see what they had fallen into.

"Wow! Look at this!" said Mathew.

There were jewels and treasure scattered everywhere on the floor of the pyramid. There were rubies, diamonds, emeralds, sapphires, topaz, gold, and silver, and other things they were unfamiliar with. The children walked over and began to touch everything; they couldn't believe it was real. Sue walked over to the open treasure chest that looked as if treasure had spilled out from it. On the very top of it was a crown and a tiara, which were covered with different colored jewels. Sue put on the tiara and turned around to Mathew and said, "It fits!" Mathew picked up the crown, which also was covered with jewels, and put it on.

"This fits too!" said Mathew smiling. They left on their crowns as they continued to explore their newfound riches.

"Sue, do you know what this means? We're rich!" exclaimed Mathew.

"Mathew, this isn't ours. Someone must know that this treasure is down here," said Sue.

"Well, we just stumbled over it. I can't imagine anyone else going through what we just did to get here. That was pretty rough," said Mathew.

"We still need to get out of here, and we can't take any of this with us because we fell pretty far down. There's no way we can carry anything," said Sue.

"I know, but can't you let a person dream a little?" asked Mathew, smiling.

Sue put the tiara back on the treasure chest and Mathew returned the crown.

"Let's try and find our way out of here," said Mathew.

"But we still don't know where this serpent is that we're supposed to find," said Sue. "We have the orb; can't we ask it?"

"That's a good idea!" Mathew picked up the orb and asked, "Where is the serpent?"

The orb changed from the blinding light to a dull gray color, and inside of it was a picture of a serpent made out of stone. The serpent had only one eye and the eye looked as though it was another orb. That orb was the color of a rainbow: reds, blues, greens, and purples.

"Can you tell where it is Mathew?" Sue asked.

"Can you show us where the serpent is?" Mathew asked the orb.

The next picture of the serpent was further away, and they could see its surroundings.

"Sue, look at that!" said Mathew. "That's where we came in. There's the sports arena, or whatever it's called, and the serpent is on the entrance of that. We need to find our way out of this pyramid."

And with that, the children did circle back, and, with some difficulty, they finally made it up and out of the pyramid. They saw the entrance and hurried for it.

When the children reached the entrance, they both stuck their heads through the doorway. They saw no dragons or anyone else.

"The plan," Mathew whispered to Sue, "is to go straight for the sports arena. Run as fast as you can. Here, take the orb," as he handed it to her. "If something happens, keep going and don't look back. I'll be fine. The eye needs to return to the serpent, and this needs to end."

Sue was scared, but she knew what she had to do. She gave Mathew a nod.

"On the count of three, we'll go," said Mathew, "One ... two ... three!"

Both Sue and Mathew took off at a run, as fast as they could go, with Sue leading the way. The sports arena was the length of a football field away, with nothing in between for cover. The children saw nothing until they got halfway there; then, they saw their mother and Sir Wilfred walking toward them. They seemed to have appeared out of nowhere. Sylvia was carrying her sword and Sir Wilfred his wand. The children ran up to them.

"Mother this is almost over," said Sue. "We'll be a family again when we give the serpent back his eye!" Sue threw her arms around her mother, but her mother did not respond like a mother should have. She held her hand out and said, "Give me the orb!" in a demanding, voice.

"Sue, get away from her!" said Mathew as he grabbed her shoulder and pulled her back away from Sylvia. "You are not our mother! Who are you?" asked Mathew who looked confused and bewildered.

"Yes, I am your mother, but I never wanted children. I was told that I had to have children in order to be Queen of my Empire. I was forced, at a very young age, to marry a man I did not love. I got pregnant quickly and gave birth to a son, then immediately became pregnant again, and had a daughter. I was so depressed and miserable. That is when I conceived the plan to rid the kingdom of my parents and build, out of the ruins, a new kingdom."

"So you are behind all of this?" asked Mathew, who could hardly believe his ears.

"Sir Wilfred, why are you letting her do this? Why don't you stop her?" asked Sue.

Sir Wilfred looked down at the ground and shuffled his feet, as if ashamed. He looked back up at the children, pointed his wand and said, "Just do as you're told and hand over the orb!"

"So, are you the one she loves? You are in this with her? You were disloyal to Quasar? How could you?" asked Sue, shaking her head in disbelief.

"When you fall in love, you will understand the power that it has," said Sir Wilfred, who still pointed his wand at the children.

Just then, Quasar appeared from out of the forest and along with him came their father, Xaviera, and Kai? *What's Kai doing with them?* wondered Mathew.

"Give me the orb, quickly!" demanded Sylvia, who started to lunge at Sue.

"Run, Sue!" yelled Mathew.

Sue took off like a bullet and ran toward the serpent, determined to not let anyone or anything get in her way.

"Stop her!" Sylvia yelled at Sir Wilfred.

Sir Wilfred pointed his wand, shooting streams of blue energy, which nearly hit Sue as she zigzagged back and forth, dodging the wand's rays. She was almost there when a dragon appeared from out of nowhere and landed right in front of her. The dragon was twice as big as Olaf or Nuri and had massive, yellowed fangs. He was dark green with big, red eyes that had black slits in them. He had bony plates along his back, down to his tail and sharp talons on top of his wings. Sue tried to run past him, but each time she tried, the dragon moved to block her way.

"You're not going anywhere, Missy," said the dragon, snarling at Sue.

"Sylvia, let her pass!" demanded Quasar. He ran to confront her.

"Not you or anyone else can give me orders. I am Queen of my Empire, and you are nothing. You shall die like the rest of the cowards that are unworthy to live!"

"That's fine; kill me, and you too shall die. Then the prince and princess shall rule the kingdom as it is written in *The Book of Wisdom*.

"Rubbish! I don't believe that nonsense. It is only myth and folklore. It is nothing to take seriously! Only fools like you and my family believe in such fairytales!" screamed Sylvia.

"What has happened to you, Sylvia? Why are you so bitter and ugly? Why have you betrayed your people?" asked Quasar, trying to understand.

"You were always their pet. They treated you better than they treated me. They never cared what happened to me; they only wanted me to have children to inherit the kingdom. They never wanted me to have anything for myself, but I showed the so-called King and Queen, who really was most powerful. I'm more powerful than any of them, and I'm even more powerful than Quasar, the Great Wolf."

"Sylvia, it wasn't like that. They loved you more than life itself. That's why your parents came to me: to keep you from dying. They knew you would die young. That's why they wanted you to marry, so that your children would rule the kingdom. Otherwise your family would have lost it, but they lost it anyway because you betrayed them.

"No! No! I am well! You saved me, and now I have your power! I am very, very strong now. I'm more powerful than you ever were!" Sylvia screamed.

"Sylvia, you are dying; you are not well. I could only keep you alive physically, but inside you have no spirit, no soul, and no heart. Without those things, you will most certainly die. No one, not even I, can live without them. Your family knew it, and this is why they wanted you to marry and have children so early," said Quasar.

"You lie! You're a liar! Just like the rest of them, and for that you will die!" Sylvia screamed. She swung her sword toward the wolf. Quasar grabbed the sword by his teeth and slung it away. Mathew watched the sword as it spun through the air, shooting purple rays of energy until it finally landed on the hard ground.

Mathew rushed for the sword, knowing that he needed to be armed so that he could help Sue, who was still cut off from the serpent by the dragon. Mathew picked up the sword and rushed toward Sue.

"Stop him!" yelled Sylvia at Sir Wilfred.

Sir Wilfred aimed his wand and wounded Mathew in the leg. Mathew screamed in excruciating pain and grabbed his leg.

"Mathew!" Sue screamed. She tried to run after him."

"Don't even try, Missy," said the dragon; he would not let her pass.

Mathew continued his pursuit while holding his leg and limping. They were too close now to give up. Mathew finally reached Sue, and in his rage he swung the sword at the dragon. The sword's purple energy knocked the dragon back. The sword was so powerful that it knocked the dragon off the ground before he came crashing down again, on his back. The ground opened and swallowed him up.

"Run Sue!" screamed Mathew.

Sue took off again, determined that this time no one was going to get in her way. It was right there. She was really close now, not knowing that Sylvia was hot on her trail and Quasar on hers.

Mathew turned around to look to see what was behind him and he saw that Kai was fighting off several wolves that had attacked him. He also saw his father and Xaviera who were also fighting several revolutionists. It looked to Mathew that they were just taking turns cutting them down. Xaviera would blast one with her wand then his father would strike one down with his sword. They seemed to be enjoying themselves. Mathew thought this was strange.

The sky had once again turned black. Mathew looked up to see a sky filled with fire-breathing dragons. He knew that Olaf and Nuri had to be up there somewhere.

He turned around to see if Sue had made it to the serpent, but a hoof struck him in the face. The centaur knocked Mathew to the ground, and he dropped the sword. Mathew shook his head to get his bearings, only to see the centaur's hooves coming down on him again. In an instant, Mathew rolled to the right, dodging the centaur's lethal weapons, but the centaur did not stop there. He continued to rear up and crash down, determined to crush Mathew. Mathew continued to roll from left to right, trying to avoid being stomped to death.

Mathew could see the sword just on the other side of the centaur and he thought that if he continued to roll, he would then be able to reach his sword.

"Where is your dragon friend now?" taunted the centaur. "He's not here to save you. Now, you must fend for yourself, if you can."

"You're a coward to attack a person from the back. I never saw you coming! How can I fight back when I have nothing to fight with?" yelled Mathew.

The centaur let up only for a moment to allow Mathew to retrieve his sword.

"Now we are even. We both have weapons," said the centaur, as he reared up to give the lethal blow. "Now let's see what you've ..."

But before the centaur could even finish his sentence Mathew swung his sword in a rage, just as he had done with the dragon, and sliced the centaur's two front hooves off. The centaur screamed in pain, and Mathew hit him again as the centaur crashed down on his haunches. The ground opened and swallowed the centaur.

Mathew looked over to see if Sue had reached the serpent yet. He could see Sue, Quasar, Sylvia, and Sir Wilfred standing just a few feet away from the serpent. Mathew started for the serpent, sword in hand. As he got closer, he could see Sir Wilfred holding his wand up to Sue's throat, and Sue was handing the eye to Sylvia.

"No!" screamed Mathew, and in his rage he swung the sword as hard as he could, hoping to hit Sir Wilfred, but instead Sue disappeared. He had hit Sue with the sword. "No!" Mathew screamed and fell to the ground, his face in his hands. He had just killed his beloved sister.

Just then a piercing howl erupted; it was as if a siren was going off. It was so loud that Mathew had to put his hands to his ears to shut out the sound. It echoed through the woods, and it seemed to bounce off the pyramids and other ruins. It seemed to be calling all the wolves, dragons, centaurs, dwarfs, unicorns, elf fairies, trolls, and other magical creatures. Fortunately for them, the sun had just set over the horizon. Within seconds after the howl, the field in which Mathew kneeled was no longer empty. It was filled with magical creatures and revolutionists.

Mathew saw Nuri and Olaf flying overhead. Nuri, with his sharp talons, swooped down and grabbed Sylvia, and Olaf grabbed Sir Wilfred. Mathew saw something drop from Sylvia's hand.

"The orb!" yelled Mathew as he got up and ran toward the orb. Fighting his way at first to make a path, he realized the creatures were actually making a path for him. They backed up and bowed down to him. It was very solemn. Only the sounds of breathing could be heard.

Suddenly he felt a hand on his right shoulder. To his surprise his father and Xaviera stood next to him. Mathew embraced his father and whispered in his ear, "I killed Sue." He sobbed uncontrollably.

When his crying slowed, William pulled Mathew's head away from his and looked into his eyes. "Mathew," he said. "It was an accident. You didn't mean to. Things like this happen in war when adrenalin is flowing and things are moving at a very fast pace. I know you didn't mean to hurt her. You loved her." And with that said they both walked hand in hand together with Xaviera, toward the orb.

The orb glowed rainbow colors as it always had. Mathew bent down and picked it up and walked toward the serpent, where Quasar and Kai stood.

"You have done well Mathew," said Quasar, smiling at Mathew.

"How can you say that? I killed my sister! I wish we had never helped you. All this has been a waste. I should have listened to Sue; she wanted to go home. She never wanted to help you. I should have listened to her," said Mathew as he continued to sob.

"You did what your heart told you to do. You and Sue did what was right. Now, restore the eye of the serpent, and see who is loyal to your throne," said Quasar.

Mathew walked to the serpent and inserted the orb. Immediately many creatures and revolutionists disappeared; they were sucked into the ground. Mathew looked over at the pyramid, and to his surprise, he began to see snakes slithering down the northern side of the pyramid and into the ground. He looked up to look for his mother and Sir Wilfred, but Nuri's and Olaf's talons were empty. His mother and Sir Wilfred were gone. About one third of the creatures and revolutionists were gone, including some dragons. Quasar, William, Xaviera, and Kai stood with Mathew, next to the serpent.

"So, I guess everyone left is loyal to the throne, is that right?" asked Mathew.

"Yes, but we are still missing one," said Quasar.

"Who's that?"

The ground began to shake where Mathew stood, and the earth began to crumble, like something was burrowing its way out. Mathew jumped aside and watched the ground become a hole, and from out of the hole something was trying to escape. As Mathew continued to watch he could tell that it was a person, but with all the dirt he couldn't tell who it was until finally the person rose up, and the ground came back together as if nothing had come through.

"Sue!" yelled Mathew as he knelt down to hold her. "I thought I killed you! Thank goodness you're alive," said Mathew sobbing.

"I'm alright, I felt something hit my legs and then the next thing I knew I was in the dark," said Sue, getting to her feet.

"Why didn't Sue die?" asked Mathew to Quasar. "Not that I wanted her to die, of course," he said, smiling at Sue.

"Sylvia's sword is made of magic. She could not kill anyone with it. It can only be used to restrain people using trees, or the ground, if there are no trees," said Quasar.

"How come everything stopped when I hit Sue with the sword?" asked Mathew.

"The howl that I cried is the 'Call of the Beast.' Everyone knows that when they hear that, something bad had just happened to the royal family. The last time they heard that was ten years ago, when the revolt took place. It calls everyone together from miles around," said Quasar.

As Quasar looked out into the crowd, there were thousands of creatures and people. "Yes, these are your people, Your Majesties," said Quasar, as he bowed his head. The rest of the crowd followed, which included, Kai, Xaviera and their father.

Mathew's and Sue's heads were immediately adorned with the crowns that they had seen in the pyramid.

Mathew and Sue stood there looking out into the crowd; they felt the joy and sorrow of everything that they had been through. It was actually coming to an end, or was it only a beginning?

"Quasar, how did Kai get out of the prison that we made from the cord? We thought that he was the one who betrayed the royals and who started the revolt?" asked Sue.

"Ah, yes, that is what I wanted you to believe. The cord was a fake; only the dwarfs can make a real magic cord that is unbreakable. You see, I was puzzled. I did not know who actually started this revolt. Sylvia and Sir Wilfred displayed perfect loyalty; I did not suspect them. I used Kai as a decoy, to act as my spy," said Quasar, who looked very happy with himself. "If everyone knew that I suspected my brother, they wouldn't think that I suspected them because the culprit would have been caught. Kai also had to guard the royal jewels."

"The royal jewels! We found jewels in the pyramid! Are those our jewels?" asked Sue.

"Yes! That is where we hid them so they would not be found," said Quasar.

"Father," said Sue looking at William, "I saw you defending mother; I watched you stab a revolutionist."

"What you saw was a revolutionist that Sylvia had ordered to kill me; after I killed him, Sir Wilfred saw you and Mathew being carried away by Olaf, and they fled to pursue you," said William. "That's when I knew for sure that Sylvia and Sir Wilfred had started the revolt."

"Quasar, how come Sir Wilfred and Sylvia didn't stop us from breaking the spell that the witch had put on you?" asked Sue.

"Because of her greed; she was not satisfied with the jewels she had access to. She wanted all the jewels. You see, before the royals were killed, the King, Queen, and I agreed to hide what jewels we could because we suspected a revolt was coming. Sylvia knew that she needed me alive and well to retrieve them. She was not involved in the hiding of the jewels because of her health; her parents thought that she did not need the added burden," said Quasar, with bitterness.

"Master Quasar, how did you know to put a riddle inside the orb when nothing had happened yet?" asked Sue curiously.

"When I went to see the witch, long ago, before she cursed me, I knew that she would betray me, but as it turned out, I was wrong. It was not the witch, but the beloved princess and my so-called trusted servant, Sir Wilfred, who betrayed me. I had to make sure that the kingdom would survive somehow, so I had to have a final spell in place that, once unlocked, would set things back as they had been. You see, I couldn't prevent any of this from happening, but I could fix it once it had."

"So what now?" asked Mathew.

"Now it is up to you! You and Sue are giving orders now! You tell us!" said Quasar, as he looked out into the crowd.

Mathew and Sue looked at each other, and then shrugged their shoulders. Mathew shouted, "Party!"

The crowd, upon hearing the order, immediately began cheering, singing, and dancing. They were celebrating the end of ten years of war and their hopes of everlasting peace with their new leaders, the Royal Highnesses, Mathew and Sue.

As the day finally ended and Mathew and Sue found themselves back in their beds, they couldn't help but wonder, was it all a dream? When they woke, would they find themselves in their beds in their cabin, or would they find themselves in this wonderful new world where magical creatures actually existed? Was Quasar real, or was he a figment of their imaginations? Only time would tell, for they would soon be overcome by sleep, and maybe, just maybe, they would awaken to a new world where even more strange creatures existed. But for now, farewell.

The End ...

or just the beginning?

Printed in the United States
217103BV00001B/16/P